Freedom's Compass

Isla Montgomery

Freedom's Compass

Dedication

To my husband, my best friend and family, whose support is the bedrock of my life.

The book is a testament to the power of love, the resilience one finds within, and the enduring spirit of hope that blossoms even amidst despair – never quietened. It's also dedicated to those who've fought against seemingly insurmountable odds, to those whose laughter echoes even in the darkest of times, a reminder that even in the face of a world saturated with shadowy conspiracies, love, laughter, an unwavering belief in the human spirit can and will prevail. This is for all those who dare to believe we are free, to love, and to laugh, even when the odds are stacked against them. To the dreamers, the lovers. I hope this story resonates with the strength of your own spirits and that you find in its pages a reflection of your own indomitable human heart.

Introduction

In the heart of the idyllic countryside, where rolling hills meet quaint villages, and the aroma of freshly baked scones hangs heavy in the air, lies a secret far more sinister than any sleepy hollow might suggest. This is not your typical countryside idyll, this is the setting for a conspiracy that is far-reaching and technologically advanced. What begins as unsettling quirks quickly escalates into a chilling mystery, leading to a perilous journey.

A Change in Air

The small town of Greenpool, a picturesque town of cottages and bungalows, rows of terraces and manicured green spaces, was nestled within rolling hills, yet only a few miles inland from the endless stretch of ocean. A place of simple contentment for its inhabitants, a community where the children run around laughing with their grandparents and friends.

Their neighbourhood was on the outskirts, a semi-village in its own right, and the kind of place where neighbours could chat more than a simple passing hello. They looked out for each other and had a general sense of ease and relaxation. They had cafes, restaurants, pubs, independent shops, green spaces, schools and a church, all within walking distance. Surrounding the area were fields filled with crops and miles of forests, pretty lakes and within driving distance of the City's bright lights.

The biggest excitement was the frequent Church fetes, which brought in revellers from all over. It was a chance to showcase artisan foods, vintage and antique wares, artistic creations and live bands, and a chance for people to meet genuine friends. But lately, a subtle unease had begun to creep into Eleanor Vance's comfortable existence. It wasn't anything dramatic, nothing that could be pinned down or easily explained: more a feeling, a change in the air.

It started subtly, with small, almost imperceptible alterations in the routines of those closest to her. Her husband, Warrick, had become strangely withdrawn. He spent long hours in his study, the only sound emanating from within the gentle tap-tap-tap of his keypad, interrupted only by the occasional sigh, heavy with unspoken anxieties. His normally light-hearted banter had been replaced by a quiet solemnity that bordered on melancholy. His usually well-groomed dark, curly hair was slightly dishevelled. His soulful eyes had taken on a strained, almost distant look. He was always up before her but lately, he was going to bed earlier and waking up later.

The other thing she noticed was that he'd stopped saying "morning beautiful" with his gorgeous smile and eyes, which told her he loved her. Her unease was partly that she didn't feel beautiful of late, she felt off. She'd always ensured her strawberry blonde locks were long, straightened and glossy, but she'd noticed her hair was getting thinner – was it stress or age-related? Her sparkling blue eyes were showing the signs of age in the form of feint lines. They usually got up, got showered and then went for a jog or walk and although she still managed to get a good walk or jog to maintain her petite frame, Warrick wasn't joining her much.

Then there was Maeve, their elderly neighbour, a woman whose daily routine was as predictable as the sunrise. Maeve's attire was always immaculate, floral and her make-up appeared air brushed. She looked young for her years and what she lacked in decorum at times, she made up for in having the most beautiful garden and home in the area, hands down. She was the keeper of the neighbourhood's collective memory, the one who knew every family secret and every scandalous rumour, but she could keep secrets as though her life depended on it. She wasn't a gossip; she was very sharp, and she'd become strangely disoriented. She'd started forgetting things, simple everyday occurrences like where she'd left her spectacles or what day it was. Her once sharp wit, usually laced with a healthy dose of sardony, had dulled, replaced by a disconcerting quietude. Her beautiful garden filled with roses, usually a riot of vibrant colour, was neglected, wilting under the summer sun. Even young Ashton, the baker's son, whose life revolved around football and girls - seemed subdued. His usual neat, short fair hair was left to grow long, his light brown eyes taking on a solemn glaze, and his boisterous laughter was absent, replaced by a quiet brooding that sat ill on his rosy cheeks. His once meticulously organised shop displays were now a mixed bag of bread and pies displayed together without thought. His usual creative wit in writing specials for the day with the words "spot the spelling mistake here and win a free pack of doughnuts" was replaced with a simple drawing of a doughnut – it was weird.

Eleanor, perceptive and sensible in nature, initially dismissed these changes as stress. The pressures of modern life, the relentless march of technology, and the anxieties of the ever-changing world – they were taking their toll. She reasoned that it was merely a temporary blip, a collective sigh of the times. She even considered purchasing a self-help book on managing stress, something with a soothing title and a reassuring cover. But something gnawed at her, a persistent, uncomfortable feeling that went beyond the usual humdrum anxieties of daily life.

The first genuinely unsettling event occurred during a seemingly innocuous afternoon tea with Maeve. Armed with a plate of her famous ginger biscuits, Eleanor had gone to visit her neighbour, finding her slumped over a half-finished crossword, a look of profound bewilderment etched onto her face. The crossword itself was utterly abandoned, an unfinished mess of scribbled letters and frustrated sighs. This wasn't unusual in itself; Maeve often struggled with the cryptic clues. What unsettled Eleanor was the small, intricately carved wooden bird that lay perched on Maeves' lap. It was a beautiful thing, a tiny carving of a kingfisher, its feathers exquisitely detailed. Eleanor knew the bird; it belonged to her, a cherished souvenir from a trip to Istanbul.

How it had ended up in Maeves' possession, she couldn't fathom.

A couple of days later, the aroma of burnt fried eggs hung heavy in the air, a fitting metaphor for the morning unfolding in Warrick and Eleanor's otherwise sleek and sophisticated kitchen. Warrick, usually the epitome of cheerful morning energy, stared blankly at his reflection in the darkened chrome of the coffee machine, leaving the eggs to burn. He'd been laid off.

Not fired, not downsized – *laid off.*

A euphemism that felt as hollow as the promise of a generous severance package he hadn't yet received.

His normal morning of jogging with Eleanor and Winston, their Irish wolfhound, was replaced with a sombre desire to be alone.

Eleanor attempted to lighten the mood. "Well," she chirped, forcing a smile that didn't quite reach her eyes, "at least we can finally tackle the renovation we've been avoiding!" Her words, intended to be reassuring, hung in the silence like a misplaced note in a symphony. They'd moved back to her home town following a series of setbacks and the plan had been to renovate properties, leading to a viable new business endeavour. But their plans had been changed for them, and they'd adapted as always. And the carefree energy that usually filled their mornings felt replaced by a subtle, pervasive unease. This wasn't just a bad day; it was the tremor before the earthquake.

The thought flickered in Warrick's mind to head to his photography studio in the garden to check on his new developments, but he couldn't muster the will and energy to pull himself away from the frown lines he noticed in his reflection.

Eleanor walked into the kitchen, lifted the eggs off the induction cooker and set them aside to be served to the wildlife they fed. She prepared a new batch for them and touched her husband's back in comfort.

Her mind wandered to a few weeks prior, which had been riddled with smaller, seemingly insignificant oddities. A mysterious charge on their credit card, a letter in the post addressed to someone else but with their address on it, a delayed shipment of Eleanor's make-up (a catastrophe of epic proportions in her world), packages delivered with delivery proof photos inside someone's bin, and a series of increasingly bizarre spam emails promising everything from cheap therapy to suspiciously cheap vacations to places she'd been dreaming of visiting.

Individually, these incidents might have been dismissed as mere annoyances, but collectively, they whispered a disquieting narrative of something amiss.

Eleanor, attuned to subtle patterns, felt a prickle of unease.

Warrick, however, remained firmly rooted in the realm of rational explanation. "Bad luck," he'd shrugged it off, "a string of coincidences."

But the job loss was a different beast altogether. Warrick, a successful engineer, had been a pillar of stability, his career a testament to his dedication and hard work.
Losing his job wasn't just a financial blow; it struck at the core of his identity. Being the only breadwinner was tough. Eleanor's most recent job ended a few months prior and she had been unable to find anything since. A half-finished renovation looming without the funds to pay for it. The carefully constructed edifice of their lives, built on mutual support and shared aspirations, suddenly seemed very shaky, the foundation shifting beneath their feet.

The job market for Warrick's line of work was being squeezed into a single sector, one devoid of individuality and requiring additional responsibilities for the same or less pay, a pattern he'd noticed for a few years after his previous job loss a few years before that when they nearly went bankrupt. And he was becoming more resigned at the thought of attending interviews and the upheaval of a possible move to a different region if he couldn't find anything locally.

The day continued in a similarly unsettling rhythm. The bank called, informing them of a series of inexplicable payments, leaving their account teetering on the brink of zero. Warrick's attempts to resolve the issue were met with robotic indifference, each conversation ending in a frustrating loop of automated responses and transferred calls.

He felt like a fly caught in a spiderweb, each desperate struggle only tightening the threads of bureaucratic entanglement.

Eleanor, meanwhile, who'd found herself increasingly drawn to online forums and news articles that hinted at something far more sinister, was gripped in an endless search that day. Whispers of manipulated markets targeted unemployment, and a growing wave of inexplicable suicides began to form a disturbing pattern. She dismissed it initially as sensationalism, yet the sheer volume of unsettling reports in various online publications, the uncanny echoes in their own misfortunes, ignited a spark of suspicion that refused to be extinguished.

That evening, curled up on the sofa amidst a growing mountain of unread emails and unanswered phone calls, Eleanor confronted Warrick. "Something's not right, Warrick," she said her voice barely a whisper. "It's not just bad luck. It feels...orchestrated."
Warrick, his face etched with exhaustion, sighed, his usual easy demeanour replaced by a weary resignation. "Eleanor, I know things are tough, but you're letting this get to you. We'll figure it out. We always do." His words, intended to comfort, instead felt like a fragile shield against a looming storm. He dismissed her concerns, his scepticism offering a strange counterpoint to her growing trepidation – a darkly comedic dissonance in their shared predicament. Their arguments, usually punctuated by laughter and affectionate teasing, now carried an undercurrent of tension, a silent acknowledgment of the cracks appearing in their seemingly comfortable world.

A few days later brought a new low.

The disappearance of Winston, their beloved Irish wolfhound. Winston, a creature of habit and unwavering loyalty, had a particular fondness for his designated sleeping spot beneath the oak tree in the garden.

But for three whole days, he was nowhere to be found.

Eleanor and Warricks' search turned up nothing; they'd put up signs everywhere on the outskirts of town, around their neighbourhood. Eleanor organised meets with a few locals to walk into the countryside to call out Winston's name, hoping he'd somehow feel the vibrations or smell them. Winston was partially deaf, born that way, but because they'd raised him from a pup, they'd trained him to stay close to them and learn their scent to return home. He would frequently take himself for walks around the countryside; their property wasn't fenced off, and he was always responsible. However, this disappearance for three days left Eleanor and Warrick feeling sick to their stomachs.

Winston wouldn't have left his loving home...he was taken.

As the strange occurrences piled up, Eleanor began to question her sanity. Was she losing her mind? Was this a collective hallucination, a bizarre ripple effect of living in a small community? She consulted Dr. Finch, her GP, a delightful man with a fondness for bad jokes. But he offered nothing more than a diagnosis of "overworked nerves", anxieties of a mind too sharp for its own good, the ramblings of a woman overburdened by the mundane, and a prescription for rest.

But Eleanor's unease deepened. She started noticing things, subtle things that others seemed to miss, or perhaps chose to ignore. She'd overhear hushed conversations in the pub, local restaurants, and shops, cryptic exchanges that trailed off abruptly when she approached. She'd see shadowy figures moving between the houses, their faces obscured by the darkness of the twilight hours. And then there were the meetings, clandestine gatherings in the old stone quarry on the other side of town, shrouded in secrecy and a palpable sense of unease. The air itself seemed to thrum with hidden energy, an unspoken tension that prickled the hairs on the back of her neck.

Strange Days

She found herself replaying the events of the previous week in her mind. The vicar, Reverend Peters, usually prone to lengthy anecdotes about God's green acres, had been unusually quiet, his eyes shadowed and distant. He'd mumbled something about "unseen forces" during their brief conversation after the evening service, a phrase that had hung in the air like the scent of woodsmoke on a damp autumnal day. She'd dismissed it then, putting it down to the late hour and the vicar's notorious fondness for a rather strong elderflower cordial. Now, however, the comment resonated with an uncomfortable significance.

Then there was Mrs Danes, the gossip extraordinaire, who'd been spotted whispering frantically with Mr Abernathy, the retired colonel known for his meticulously manicured lawn and even more meticulously guarded secrets. Usually, Mrs. Danes' pronouncements were as predictable as the setting sun, her pronouncements on matters both trivial and important delivered with the same unwavering gusto. But this hushed conversation, observed from behind the lace curtains of Eleanor's living room window, felt clandestine, secretive, laced with a tension that vibrated in the air. The usual voluble flow of gossip had inexplicably dried up. It was as if a hush had fallen over Green pool, a collective holding of breath, a shared awareness of something amiss.

Later that morning, following another extensive search of the local area calling Winston's name to no avail, she returned home to a series of bizarre messages on her phone. One from her mother, telling her to call her urgently. The next call was from Penelope, her long-time friend, who said she needed a proper chat and to call her when she could. Then an anonymous call suggested the dog was safe and to stop looking. Seriously rattled, she called her mother first. She sounded irritated and told her to get over Winston and to go out and buy a new dog in a callous-sounding way. It was completely out of character for her mother. She couldn't retrieve the number from the caller, who blatantly admitted he had Winston, and in her haste, she accidentally deleted the voicemail.

The call and voice messages left Eleanor shaken. She couldn't share any of that with Warrick whilst he had so much going on already, so she resolved herself to busy herself in the garden. It was there she noticed another anomaly. Her gardening shears, usually kept in their designated spot in the shed, were missing. Again, a seemingly insignificant detail, yet another piece in the unsettling puzzle. The feeling of unease deepened, transforming into a low-level anxiety that clung to her like the clinging mist that often shrouded the town in the early mornings.

It wasn't just the unsettling changes in the towns' behaviour, Winston, bizarre messages, and items going missing. There was a patten emerging.

There was also the matter of young Ashton, the baker's son. Typically brimming with youthful energy, he had become withdrawn, spending most of his time indoors, his once cheerful face shadowed with an inexplicable melancholy. His absence from his usual sports club, where he would usually engage in boisterous football and cricket games, was particularly striking. The usually vibrant town, a hub of activity, now felt strangely empty.

As she pondered these disturbing occurrences, Eleanor felt a growing conviction that something sinister was afoot in Greenpool. It wasn't a matter of isolated incidents; a pattern was emerging, a series of seemingly unconnected events that, when viewed together, painted a deeply disturbing picture. The whispers were no longer faint and indistinct but rather a cacophony of unheard voices, a constant, low hum beneath the surface of town life.

She fell on her knees in her garden and felt her throat constrict, stifling a tear. What on earth was happening? Where was their Winston?

That evening, while preparing dinner, Eleanor returned the call to her friend, Penelope. Penelope, an artistic creator in The City, originally from North Africa, with skin the colour of oiled mahogany and an equally enchanting face, a woman who possessed an encyclopedic knowledge of herbal remedies and conspiracy theories in roughly equal measure. She'd met Penelope at one of the jobs she'd held down for more than a few months. Penelope, naturally, had a far more dramatic interpretation. And with little time for small town quaintness, sounded agitated.

"Eleanor," she said, her voice tight with concern, "You wouldn't believe what's been happening in the city. People… disappearing. Vanishing without a trace. The police are baffled." Penelope's tone held a tremor of fear that chilled Eleanor to the bone. It wasn't just Greenpool; something far more

widespread, something far more sinister, seemed to be at play.
"Do you think Winston has disappeared the same way as the people in The City?" Penelope asked.
"I think he was taken." the words hung in the air.
"You'll find him, babe. I know you will."

Eleanor's thoughts raced, the seemingly disparate events in Greenpool suddenly coalescing into a coherent, terrifying narrative. The missing objects, the unusual behaviours, the furtive meetings, Winston's disappearance and then people in The City too, even the vicar's cryptic pronouncements, weren't random occurrences; they were interconnected, forming a picture of unsettling events hinting at something far larger, far more insidious.

Winston, her loyal wolfhound, would've usually sensed her anxiety. His normally expressive eyes, usually full of playful mischief, would have comforted her and she missed him.
Eleanor's research intensified. She devoured news articles, scientific journals, and obscure online forums, piecing together the fragments of a terrifying puzzle. The seemingly disparate incidents – the job losses, the financial setbacks, the creepy recent events, and now Winston's disappearance – began to align, forming a disturbing pattern of calculated destruction. The terrifying precision of their misfortune felt both surreal and calculated.

Her late nights spent hunched over her laptop, fuelled by copious amounts of sweetened coffee and a growing sense of disquiet, were punctuated by Warrick's increasingly frustrated attempts to understand her growing obsession. He saw it as a flight into paranoia, a desperate attempt to find meaning in a series of unfortunate events. She was determined to disprove his scepticism, however, to show him the weight of the accumulating evidence. He couldn't dismiss the string of events as mere coincidence anymore.

The sheer number of misfortunes, their precisely timed arrival, and her sudden awareness of it all couldn't simply be ignored. One late night, while browsing a particularly obscure scientific forum, Eleanor stumbled upon a mention of experimental nanotechnology, a substance capable of manipulation of human behaviour and emotions. The implications hit her with the force of a physical blow. The manipulated news reports, the strangely altered social media trends, the bizarre behaviour of their friends and neighbours - it all began to make terrifying sense. The unseen hand guiding their misfortune was far more sophisticated than anything she could have imagined.

The realisation struck her with the chilling clarity of a winter sunrise – they weren't victims of bad luck. They were targets. Targets of an unseen conspiracy enacted with terrifying precision. The weight of this realisation settled on her shoulders, heavy and suffocating. Sleep became a distant memory, replaced by a constant, niggling anxiety that permeated every aspect of her life. The seemingly placid life she had painstakingly built with Warrick was unravelling, thread by thread, leaving them exposed to a malevolent force that operated in the shadows. The cracks, once subtle and almost imperceptible, had widened into gaping fissures, threatening to swallow them whole. The first domino had fallen, and the rest were poised to follow.

And then Winston returned home, but he was thin and bedraggled, with a haunted look in his usually playful eyes. Where had he been? Eleanor was convinced someone had taken him, and he'd obviously escaped from their clutches. They were all relieved, but his demeanour was different.

He refused his favourite carrot sticks, the aroma of which usually sent him into paroxysms of joyful tail-thumping. He also developed a peculiar habit of staring intently at the old stone well in the garden, whimpering softly as if he had sensed something deeply disturbing.

His behaviour, usually predictable to the point of predictability, was increasingly erratic, unsettling, and profoundly worrying. His usual exuberance was replaced by a strange and unnerving anxiety. Instead of wanting to be outside, he took to hiding behind the sofa and whining softly, a low, mournful sound that tugged at her heartstrings. Eleanor, feeling a heightened sense of disquiet, decided she could no longer ignore the unsettling events unfolding around her.

The quiet contentment of Greenpool was gone, replaced by a chilling sense of unease. The whispers were no longer mere whispers; they were a chorus of foreboding, a harbinger of something terrible about to unfold. She knew, with an unnerving certainty, that her life and the lives of those she loved, were about to be irrevocably changed. The events of recent weeks, specifically, had opened the door to a world of secrets, which she was now determined to explore, even if it meant facing the real possibility of her own demise. The quiet town was anything but quiet anymore, and Eleanor, armed with nothing but her intuition and a creeping dread, was about to find herself right at its epicentre. The clock was ticking. And Greenpool held its breath.

The idyllic charm had crumbled, revealing a dark, menacing underbelly. The truth was out there, hidden in plain sight, waiting to be discovered. And Eleanor, despite her apprehension, was ready to find it. The ordinary was becoming extraordinary, the familiar strangely unfamiliar. The unsettling thoughts, once faint and indistinct, now seemed to be growing louder, more insistent, weaving themselves into the framework of her existence.

Eleanor, increasingly convinced that something profoundly amiss was going on in Greenpool, began to piece together the fragments of her observations. The misplaced objects, the unusual behaviours, the furtive meetings, Winston's peculiar anxieties and the people missing in The City were all connected. A hidden truth lay buried beneath the placid surface of her beloved town, and Eleanor was determined to unearth it. The quiet, vibrant contentment of Greenpool was shattered, replaced by a growing sense of dread.

Questions

The unsettling silence of the following days was disturbing, to say the least. Warrick, still reeling from his job loss, remained stubbornly sceptical of Eleanor's increasingly frantic theories. He attributed her anxiety to stress, the pressure of their dwindling finances, and the nagging fear of an uncertain future. He tried to be supportive, offering platitudes and forced smiles, but the chasm between their perceptions widened with each passing hour. Eleanor, however, felt the tightening grip of dread like a physical presence, a suffocating weight that pressed down on her chest, stealing her breath.

It started subtly. A news report about a sudden surge in accidents was brushed off as a statistical anomaly by the government's scientific researcher of noted importance, Dr Evelyn Reed. Then, a series of bizarre social media posts from friends and acquaintances, filled with oddly upbeat pronouncements about their newfound acceptance of crippling debt or sudden, inexplicable job losses celebrated as "opportunities for growth." The tone was eerily uniform, a disturbingly cheerful acceptance of misfortune. She'd seen similar posts before, but now, connected by the thread of their own predicament, the pattern felt chillingly deliberate.

One evening, while browsing through online forums, Eleanor stumbled upon a discussion thread filled with cryptic comments about "nano-tech," "the whispers," and "the great awakening." Users described a pervasive sense of unease, feelings of disconnect from reality, and the overwhelming urge to embrace negativity. Intrigued and terrified, she followed the thread, discovering more and more accounts that mirrored her own experiences and anxieties. These were not isolated incidents; they were linked, part of a larger pattern.

That night, she found Warrick staring blankly at the television, his eyes glazed over, a vacant smile playing on his lips as a news anchor cheerfully reported on a new government initiative to promote "self-reliance and personal responsibility" in the face of crippling economic hardship. The tone, the unwavering optimism in the face of widespread suffering, sent a shiver down Eleanor's spine. It was the same unsettling cheerfulness she'd seen in her friends' social media posts. The propaganda was pervasive and ubiquitous.

Her suspicions intensified when she recalled a peculiar encounter at the local grocery store. A seemingly friendly employee had offered her a sample of a new energy bar, its packaging gleaming with promises of boosted energy and mental clarity. She had politely declined, feeling an instinctive unease, a prickling at the back of her neck that had warned her to stay away. Now, the memory felt charged with significance, the employee's overly enthusiastic demeanour suddenly seeming sinister and calculated. The friendly advice, now a veiled threat.

That night, she found a dusty, old chemistry textbook in their attic. She knew next to nothing about chemistry but recalled the whispers of nanotechnology, an almost mythical technology with potential for good or evil, a double-edged sword. She flipped through its pages, searching for anything that would explain the unsettling changes she was witnessing, the increasingly bizarre behaviour she was observing in everyone around her.

Days turned into nights, each one bringing a new wave of unsettling events. Their neighbours, usually friendly and chatty, now seemed distant and preoccupied, their conversations stilted and oddly devoid of emotion. The children on their street, once full of unrestrained energy and noise, moved with a strange, unnatural quietude, their eyes holding an unnerving stillness.

Eleanor started paying closer attention to everyone's behaviour. Lunches and dinners were no longer lighthearted discussions but interrogations about their days - in the hope of uncovering anything useful. She searched for any sign that someone else was seeing what she was seeing, aware of what was happening around them.

The news reinforced the narrative of societal harmony, of a nation facing challenges with brave acceptance and resilience. Each report felt carefully crafted, each statement deliberately chosen to subtly reinforce the desired message - an overwhelming sense of acceptance in the face of adversity. It was too perfect, too coordinated.

One evening following dinner at her mother's, an imposing house on the edge of a village close to Greenpool, she noticed some old family photo albums. She began flipping through the pages of her mother as a child, her grandfather, and her father, but unusually, no photos of her grandmother. "What happened to the photos of Esther?" she asked.

"Your grandmother? She hated having her picture taken and must have hidden them many years ago. I've never been able to locate them."

"Do you have anything of hers?"

"Possibly, I don't know, this house was once hers so there's likely things dotted around in the attic. Why? Why this sudden interest in your grandmother?"

"I realise I know so little about our family and history despite you and I being so close." she smiled a warm, reassuring smile.

"Well, take a look, but I can't imagine what you'll find up there." her mother responded.

And Eleanor, armed with an insatiable desire to know everything, went straight up to the attic and began sifting through the various boxes until she came upon an old-looking trunk with the initials E. H inscribed, which were her grandmother's initials. Inside the trunk, she found a very old, velvet-bound journal with the words "Behold, this life". Intrigued, she opened it, the brittle pages whispering secrets from the past. The journal detailed a series of bizarre events that mirrored their current predicament: inexplicable financial ruin, sudden illnesses, and even the mysterious death of a beloved pet.

A chilling revelation emerged from the faded ink. Her grandmother had suspected a conspiracy, a shadowy organisation manipulating events from behind the scenes.

She had written about a secret society that thrived on decimating people's lives, control, power, and money and that she'd discovered details of this hidden network operating in the shadows. The journal ended abruptly, the last entry marked by a sense of escalating panic and dread. Why had her mother never mentioned this to her?

Eleanor's heart pounded. Could her grandmother's experiences be connected to their current situation? Was this a generational curse, a family legacy of misfortune, or something far more harrowing? The parallels were unnerving, too precise to be mere coincidence. The more she read, the more certain she became that they weren't just victims of bad luck; her entire bloodline were targets.

Without wishing to alarm her mother, she discretely took the diary, and they said their goodbyes.

The discovery of the journal further fuelled her determination to uncover the truth. She knew they were not alone in this struggle. The whispers of conspiracy, once dismissed as paranoia, were now taking shape, coalescing into a tangible threat. She continued to piece together fragments of information, scraps of evidence pointing towards a grand conspiracy, a network of power and influence that extended far beyond their small town and her family.

One evening, as Eleanor painstakingly researched online forums, she stumbled upon an encrypted message, a coded plea for help posted in a hidden corner of a seemingly innocuous website. The message spoke of government manipulation, covert mind control techniques, and a sinister plot which ultimately creates a world of negativity. It mentioned nanotechnology, a "silent killer" slowly poisoning the minds and bodies of millions.

The message hinted at a secret organisation, a cabal of powerful individuals pulling the strings from the shadows.

Eleanor showed Warrick the message, her hands trembling. He, however, remained unconvinced, his cynicism bordering on hostility. "It's just some conspiracy theory," his voice tight with a mixture of disbelief and irritation. "People are stressed,

Eleanor. We need to focus on getting back on our feet." He failed to notice the subtle shift in her eyes. The eyes of a woman who had caught a glimpse behind the curtain and understood the terrifying truth behind the mundane reality that enveloped them. The woman knew that their fight for survival was only just beginning, a battle against an invisible enemy wielding a weapon far more malicious than guns or bombs. A weapon that silenced the soul before it could utter a word of protest. The fight was for their lives, an entire world being gently, yet surely, steered toward oblivion.

She'd always prided herself on her ability to find a logical explanation for even the most peculiar occurrences.
The initial dismissal of the strange happenings as mere coincidence, quirks of the imagination, now felt flimsy, a desperate attempt to cling to normalcy in the face of encroaching chaos. The subtle shifts in her friends' and family's behaviour, previously attributed to stress or age, now seemed far more macabre, engineered with chilling precision. Her husband, normally the picture of cheerful predictability, had become withdrawn, his usually twinkling eyes clouded with a melancholic haze. Even their dog, Winston, his usually boisterous tail drooping with an unusual despondency.

She couldn't shake the feeling that Warrick's job loss was more than just a set back in their finances. It was a deliberate act, a calculated step, another one in a seemingly endless array, designed to hurt them, to break them. It wasn't the first. The string of misfortunes that had plagued them over the past few months was too consistent to be mere coincidence. The sudden lay-off from yet another job, the inexplicable bank errors that drained their savings, the relentless harassment from debt collectors - it was all too carefully coordinated, a cruel symphony of misfortune designed to reduce them to ruins.

That night, Eleanor couldn't sleep. She lay awake, the darkness of the room amplifying her anxieties. The weight of suspicion pressed down on her, a heavy cloak that stifled her breathing. She pulled out her laptop, the glow of the screen illuminating her worried face. She started to research secret societies. She thought Warrick, despite his initial disbelief, must be starting to see the truth and that he couldn't deny the overwhelming evidence. The realisation that they were being targeted, that someone or something was systematically dismantling their lives, settled heavily upon her.

Warrick lay in bed, eyes closed but not asleep. He couldn't deny feeling his wife was teetering on the brink of madness. Her obsession with the string of unfortunate events, easily dismissed as a series of coincidences, couldn't possibly be a choreographed campaign of malice. He began to see the pattern emerging of a life with someone whose obsessive nature, always a new focus, unable to hold down a steady job and blaming some unknown shadowy group she called a "cabal" instead of taking personal responsibility, unable to see the world for what it was and get on with life the way normal people did, would inevitably push them apart. He found himself questioning his love for her. He loved her, he'd felt passion he'd never felt the moment they met and he felt they'd comfortably weathered the storms together as a formidable team. Perhaps his sudden questioning was due to the stress of his job loss. He'd noticed an increase in divorce amongst his ex-work colleagues and put it down to a bad choice in partner and he always felt quietly confident he'd chosen well. And perhaps, in some way, he'd enabled her to slip into madness. Was he somehow to blame?

The next logical step, Eleanor reasoned, was to seek professional help. Dr Finch, her GP, usually meeting with dry wit, listened patiently as Eleanor recounted her tale of the increasingly erratic behaviour of her loved ones. Dr. Finch, after a thorough examination and a slightly bewildered expression, suggested stress. "Perhaps a bit of a holiday, Eleanor? A nice holiday might do you the world of good." His suggestion, while well-intentioned, felt inadequate: a flimsy bandaid on a gaping wound.

She contacted her friend, Penelope again.
"It's the ley lines, darling," she declared. "They're out of whack. The energy is all wrong. You need a cleansing ritual, pronto. In fact, we all do. There's something 'off' going on around here, and people appear oblivious. The police aren't doing anything about those missing people, so what does that tell you? Look into the Ley Lines in your region, it's got to be something to do with that." While Penelope's theories were entertaining, they were a little out there and offered little in the way of concrete solutions.

Eleanor's frustration mounted. She needed answers, and these half-baked explanations, however colourful, were not providing them. The unsettling feeling deepened, evolving into a tangible fear that coiled around her heart, tightening its grip with each passing day. The whispers, initially faint and barely perceptible, now resonated with a disturbing clarity.
They seemed to emanate from the core of Greenpool, from the ancient stone walls of the church to the rustling leaves of the

ancient oak trees that lined the neighbourhood green. They spoke of shadows, of secrets, of a dark force at work.

The more Eleanor investigated, the more she realised the unsettling events weren't confined to her household. Other neighbours were experiencing similar anomalies. Mr Fitzwilliam, the retired antique dealer, claimed his rare collection of antique silver snuff boxes had been mysteriously rearranged, each box bearing a single, almost imperceptible scratch, devaluing them. Even the usually placid pub landlord, Mr. Sale, complained of unsettling dreams and a persistent feeling of being watched.

Eleanor found herself becoming increasingly isolated. Her attempts to discuss her concerns were met with polite dismissiveness or outright incredulity. She began to question her sanity, the weight of her fears threatening to overwhelm her. Was she losing her mind? Was this all a figment of her overactive imagination, fuelled by late-night crime documentaries and too much caffeine? Why would Mr. Sale feel he was being watched? Was she the only other person who found that statement more than a little unsettling?

Driven by a desperate need to prove she wasn't losing her mind, Eleanor turned to the local library, hoping to find some clue, some explanation, in the annals of Greenpool's history. She spent days poring over dusty tomes, meticulously tracing the village's genealogy, searching for any mention of similar events, any clue to the unsettling happenings. It was during her research that she stumbled upon an intriguing entry in the town chronicle, dated back to the 17th century. The entry described a series of strange occurrences, eerily similar to the ones she'd been experiencing. Whispers in the night, inexplicable disappearances, and a general sense of foreboding that hung heavy in the air.

The entry also mentioned a secret society, a group rumoured to possess ancient knowledge and the ability to manipulate the energies of the land. The chronicle ended abruptly, the last few pages ripped out, leaving Eleanor with more questions than answers. The reference to a secret society sent a chill over her. It was a haunting echo, something dark and powerful lurking beneath the idyllic façade of Greenpool. The whispers, she realised, were not merely figments of her imagination; they were a warning.

The unsettling anomalies, previously scattered and seemingly random, now began to coalesce, forming a disturbing pattern. Mr Fitzwilliam's snuff boxes and Mr Sale's feeling of being watched were all pieces of a larger puzzle, clues pointing towards a sinister truth. Eleanor felt a pervasive dread, a chilling premonition that the seemingly quiet town held a dangerous secret.

Deep down, she knew she couldn't ignore it any longer. She couldn't dismiss it as stress, or ley lines, or simply a bad case of the jitters. This was something far more profound. The idyllic charm was a façade, a carefully crafted illusion, concealing a truth fictitious idyllic appearances could no longer quell.

Whispers

The whispers were first dismissed as the usual gossip, the quiet murmurings of a community where everyone knew everyone else's business. But the frequency of these hushed exchanges, the palpable sense of secrecy clinging to them, was undeniably unsettling. It was as if Greenpool, her sleepy, seemingly innocuous town, was harbouring a secret, a dark undercurrent flowing beneath the placid surface of its idyllic existence.

One evening, while walking Winston along the canal path, she overheard a snippet of conversation from behind a thicket of willows. Two figures, their backs to her, were speaking in low, urgent tones. She couldn't make out the words, but the tension in their voices was palpable, a stark contrast to the gentle lapping of the river against the bank. The feeling of being watched, of being privy to something she shouldn't be, sent a jolt through her.

The next day, at the bakery, she saw the usually cheerful Mrs Higgins, the owner, huddled in a corner with Mr. Peters, the vicar. Their hushed conversation was punctuated by nervous glances toward the door, their expressions grave and concerned. Mrs Higgins, known for her bubbly nature, seemed strangely reticent, her demeanour replaced by a wary silence. Eleanor's initial instinct was to dismiss these occurrences as coincidences, the product of an overactive imagination, but the whispers persisted, weaving a tapestry of unease that was impossible to ignore. The town, once a comforting haven, now felt like a stage set for a play she didn't understand, a play with uncomfortable undertones and an unknown ending.

That night, sleep evaded her. The thoughts echoed in her mind, a chorus of hushed voices that seemed to penetrate even the deepest recesses of her dreams. She found herself staring out the window, the moonlight casting a glow across her bedroom floor, the darkness outside mirroring the unsettling darkness she felt within.

The following days brought a flurry of strange incidents. The clock tower, usually meticulously maintained, stopped abruptly. The local greengrocer, Mr Olaf, a man of unwavering routine, failed to open his shop, despite standing behind the till the door shut and a small queue gradually increasing in length.

The unsettling events prompted Eleanor to speak with her husband, Warrick. "It's just Greenpool being Greenpool, darling," he'd said, his tone laced with gentle amusement. "A bit of harmless eccentricity."
He offered a different perspective, one of scientific scepticism.
He suggested that perhaps it was a strange form of mass hysteria, a collective delusion gripping everyone. He spoke of psychological phenomena, groupthink, and the power of suggestion, drawing parallels to historical accounts of similar events. His words provided a sliver of rational explanation, but Eleanor couldn't shake the feeling that something far more was at play.

Warrick was feeling something else. He'd caught Eleanor by surprise, glancing around his study, a place she rarely ventured and when he'd asked if she'd like a cuppa, she appeared to eye him with suspicion before snappishly declining his offer. Even their seemingly casual dinners with friends were dappled with unusual questions, turning a quiet dinner of much-needed respite into a series of uncomfortable glances and apologetic mutterings about early rises for work the following day.

"It's just a phase," he told himself, even as his stomach tightened. He didn't know which part of his life felt more off balance right now, the sudden loss of employment or the fact that Eleanor was becoming more convinced each day there was someone conspiring against them.

Warrick set his coffee mug down on the counter with a little more force than he meant to, but it was hard to hide his frustration. "Eleanor, please, it's not a conspiracy. I've looked over the numbers. They're cutting back. It's not some shadowy organisation trying to control the world. It's just business." But his wife didn't even look up from her laptop, her face illuminated by an eerie glow as she scrolled through article after article, each one more outlandish than the last. "You don't get it," she replied, her voice tight. "It's a setup. They want us to be desperate." Warrick's mind was racing, trying to piece together a response that wouldn't escalate things. He loved her; he did. But these spirals... they were becoming harder to handle. Still, he couldn't leave her in this state. "Eleanor," he said softly, "you've got to trust me on this one."

Warrick sat in the car, gripping the steering wheel so tight his knuckles ached. He had a meeting lined up with an old colleague, someone who had connections that might lead to a job. But the thought of it made his stomach churn. For years, he'd built his life on logic, data, and a certain stability. Now, it felt like the ground was slipping out from under him once more as if the previous years weren't enough tension. Eleanor's paranoid ramblings had only added weight to the pressure. But he couldn't shake her words, and the logic was inescapable – he'd just been laid off from a company he'd devoted the last four years to. "You don't get laid off for no reason, and there were no warnings, no explanations. It was very abrupt," he muttered to himself.

The local library, its shelves lined with dusty tomes and forgotten histories, unearthed local legends, tales of ancient rituals and hidden societies, stories that resonated with the unsettling events unfolding around her. She discovered references to a secret society, a shadowy organisation rumoured to have manipulated events in Greenpool for centuries, wielding a power that transcended the mundane. These were not mere fairy tales; they held a chilling ring of truth.

The mid-afternoon brought rain, and while sifting through old parish records, Eleanor stumbled upon a faded photograph. It showed a group of elegantly dressed individuals, their faces obscured by shadows, standing in front of a building that bore an uncanny resemblance to the old mill on the outskirts of the town. A chilling inscription on the back of the photograph read: 'The Synarchy - Maintaining Equilibrium'.
The word 'Equilibrium' seemed to take on a double meaning. As the word lingered on her mind, she stood up and needed to balance herself as she made her way swiftly to the loo. As she studied her reflection in the mirror, the word equilibrium swirled through her thoughts, a word which hinted at a balance, used by a precarious secret order that was now, clearly, being disrupted.

Eleanor's growing unease led her to seek out Mr. Holsworth, a reclusive old man living in a dilapidated cottage on the edge of the Wolds. Mr Holsworth was known for his eccentric habits and his encyclopedic knowledge of Greenpool's history. He was a walking archive, a repository of forgotten stories and local secrets. He lived with his wife; the two never had children but seemed content. He listened patiently to Eleanor's account, his eyes twinkling with a mixture of amusement and understanding. He confirmed the existence of 'The Synarchy' but offered little else except a cryptic warning.

"They're not what they seem, my dear," he rasped, his voice as dry as autumn leaves. "And their equilibrium is about to shatter." That word again, a word they'd taken on and given a double meaning to.

That evening, they were in the kitchen together. Warrick sat at the kitchen table, watching Eleanor on her laptop, her eyes wide with anxiety. Winston, usually calm, had been barking at nothing a few moments earlier, and when he'd opened the back door, there was only the sound of rain hitting the water butt. "There's nothing there, Winston. It's just the pattern of rain," he said, stroking his wiry fur.

Warrick's mind, so accustomed to equations and blueprints, struggled to solve this. "It's just stress," he thought. "Stress and a bit too much media." But he couldn't ignore the faint sense of unease that had started to take root. Eleanor had a point - just not the one she thought. People were acting strange. Jobs were disappearing. And the more he tried to make sense of the mess, the more his mind slipped into uncomfortable places. He wasn't sure if the world was getting more chaotic or if he was just starting to see it for the first time. "I'm tired of this," he muttered to himself. The exhaustion was real, the weight of both his job loss and Eleanor's spiralling thoughts starting to feel like two separate burdens, slowly crushing him from opposite sides. He needed to make a decision soon: face the chaos with the same determination he always had, or let it pull him under. "I'm going to hit the sack. Are you coming?" he asked Eleanor.

"I'll be up in a minute," she replied without turning from the screen.

Days bled into nights, and the whispers intensified. The once charming buzz was now a pervasive atmosphere of fear and uncertainty. Eleanor found herself unable to tear herself away from investigating the goings on – whilst her friends and neighbours were seemingly lost in a fog of apathy and disorientation. She felt like she was navigating unearthed secrets, each turn leading to a new revelation, each whispered conversation unveiling a deeper layer of deception. The line between reality and illusion blurred. The idyllic façade of Greenpool was crumbling, revealing a chilling reality beneath.

One evening, as she walked Winston along the familiar path by the river, she saw a figure emerge from the shadows. It was a woman, her face partially hidden by a hat, with fiery red hair that cascaded down her shoulders like a molten river. Her emerald eyes, sharp and intelligent, met Eleanor's. The woman introduced herself as Seraphina, someone who'd noticed Eleanor looking into the same things she was. She confessed that the Synarchy wasn't merely a shadowy organisation; it was a network controlling events that held immense power, and even speaking of it could mean disaster. She'd been trying to leave the network, and when she began watching the community, she noticed Eleanor, specifically, was potentially researching the goings on. Seraphina, long since seeking redemption from her unfortunate upbringing, offered Eleanor her help, promising to reveal the Synarchy's plans and assist in dismantling their nefarious operation. She spoke briefly of ancient energies and sophisticated technology, of a complex web of manipulation that reached far beyond the boundaries of Greenpool. This was no longer a simple small-town mystery but a battle against a formidable enemy.

The Dog's Suspicions

Winston was not known for his subtlety. He was a dog of unwavering opinions, expressed primarily through enthusiastic tail wags (for treats and walks), low growls (for the postman and vacuum cleaner), and a disconcerting ability to sniff out a dropped sausage roll from fifty paces. But ever since his forced disappearance - she knew he wouldn't have run off like that; he was off. His usually boisterous enthusiasm was muted, replaced by an air that bordered on the surly.

It started subtly. A missed treat or two. A reluctance to join in his usual game of "fetch" with his squeaky ball. Then, the staring. At first, Eleanor dismissed it as the onset of old age. Winston was, after all, pushing twelve – a respectable age, even for his breed. But then came the nightmares. Every night, he would let out little whimpers in his sleep, his paws paddling frantically as if he were swimming in treacle.

He'd wake with a start, eyes wide, panting softly, and then, come the morning, resume his post at the base of the oak, staring.

The oak tree. It was a magnificent specimen, its gnarled branches reaching towards the heavens. It had stood for centuries, a silent witness to the comings and goings of generations in Greenpool. Eleanor had always admired its stoic beauty, but now, looking at it through Winston's watchful eyes, a sense of unease settled in her stomach. There was something about it, a palpable energy that seemed to hum in the air around its ancient trunk.

One afternoon, while Eleanor was attempting to coax Winston into a game of "chase the ball" (which he ignored), she noticed something peculiar. He wasn't just staring at the tree; he was sniffing it. Not a casual sniff, either. This was a deep, probing sniff he reserved for particularly enticing smells, like discarded fish and chips or the freshly baked bread from Higgins' bakery. His little black nose twitched, his ears pricked, and he let out a soft, almost inaudible whine. He then proceeded to dig furiously at the base of the tree, sending a shower of earth and loose leaves flying.

Intrigued, Eleanor knelt beside him. She helped him shift the soil, revealing a small, intricately carved wooden box buried in the ground. It was ancient-looking, its surface covered in a layer of moss and grime. As Eleanor carefully lifted it from its hiding place, she felt a strange vibration, a low hum that resonated through her hands. She opened the box cautiously. A single, tarnished silver box lay inside, nestled on a bed of faded velvet. The box was small, no bigger than her thumbnail. It was engraved with a strange symbol – a circle intersected by two lines, forming a sort of X. The symbol was unfamiliar, yet it stirred a deep, unsettling feeling within her. It felt…wrong.

As she held the box, the humming intensified, and a sudden wave of dizziness washed over her. She stumbled back, dropping the box onto the grass.

Winston, sensing her distress, nudged her hand with his wet nose, his brown eyes filled with an uncanny intelligence. He whined again, a sound that seemed to convey both warning and understanding. He seemed to be communicating something beyond the usual canine repertoire of barks and whines. It was as if he understood the significance of the silver box, the danger it represented.

Eleanor's initial fear gave way to a surge of adrenaline. This wasn't just a strange occurrence but a confirmation of her growing suspicion. The whispers, the strange behaviours of her neighbours, people disappearing in The City, the unsettling dreams – it all pointed towards something sinister, an undercurrent unnoticed by those around her. And now, her faithful companion, Winston, was inexplicably caught up in it.

She picked up the box, carefully placing the small silver box inside. She knew she couldn't leave it there. The humming had been unnerving; the symbol was disturbing.

That evening, Eleanor examined the box under a magnifying glass, turning it this way and that. The silver was tarnished, obscuring the finer details of the engraving. She cleaned it gently with a soft cloth, revealing more of the intricate design. The two lines crossing the circle were not straight lines but subtly curved, almost like snakes entwined. And within the circle itself, she noticed a tiny inscription – a series of seemingly random letters and symbols. It looked almost like a code.

The discovery of the box and Winston's unusual behaviour had thrown Eleanor even deeper into the enigma of The Synarchy. The thoughts were no longer just a background hum but a deafening roar, a symphony of secrets and lies that threatened to consume her entire world. She knew that she had to decipher the mystery of the box, uncover the meaning of the inscription, and most importantly, understand why her dog, a creature of simple pleasures, seemed to be privy to a hidden truth that even she was struggling to comprehend.

The next morning, Eleanor decided to seek advice from the local historian, Mr. Holsworth. He listened patiently as Eleanor recounted the story of the box, Winston's unusual behaviour, and her growing suspicions about The Synarchy. He listened intently, his eyes twinkling with a mixture of fascination and concern. His eyes widened when she showed him the box and described the strange symbol.

"That," he said, his voice low and grave, "is the mark of the Old Ones."

He explained that the symbol was an ancient emblem, associated with a powerful energy said to be capable of manipulating time and space. He spoke of forgotten rituals and clandestine societies that had worshipped this energy for centuries. The Synarchy, he speculated, was merely a modern manifestation of these ancient cults, employing advanced technology to harness the power of the Old Ones for their own nefarious purposes. He also suggested that Winston's sensitivity might stem from a heightened sense of energy, a sensitivity to the ancient energies that The Synarchy was wielding. Dogs, he explained, were often more attuned to such things than humans.

Mr. Holsworth provided another alarming revelation that vast amounts of exotic or negative energy could, if captured, produce a phenomenon similar to time travel. He gave Eleanor a few old books on local lore, suggesting she look for any references to the symbol and the Old Ones. He also gave her the name of an old professor, Professor Collings, who was very clued up about the possibilities of time travel.

He warned her, however, that this was a dangerous path she was treading, a path fraught with peril and uncertainty. But

Eleanor, armed with the knowledge gained from Mr. Holsworth, was ready to face the darkness that loomed over Greenpool.

The race against time had accelerated. Eleanor realised that the Synarchy wasn't just manipulating individuals; they were manipulating the very flow of time, using some advanced technology and energies from the Old Ones. Every moment was critical. The whispers had become screams. And she had a feeling that Winston's peculiar behaviour might be the key to unlocking the secrets that could save them all. The old oak tree the box - they were all pieces of a puzzle that, once solved, could reveal a terrifying truth about The Synarchy and its sinister plans. But, for now, it was a race against time - a race Eleanor was determined to win, for her town, her family, and everyone else caught up in their disturbing plot.

A Meeting

She arranged to meet with Professor Collings.

The day she met the professor, she'd relayed all she knew of what she'd heard.

"For the sake of argument, let's say we had the knowledge to determine what's required to build a time machine but we lack the resources for the build. Technically, if we discovered a way to produce those resources, we could build the machine. Our best research indicates the machine requires exotic or, rather, negative energy. All the matter we know of and can see in the world around us is positive energy. If we can theoretically create negative energy, it would only be possible in small quantities, which would be insufficient for a viable machine. It's not impossible, but there is a limit on our current technology and understanding of quantum mechanics and this is the sticking point at present."

"I won't presume to understand what negative and positive energy are but if this has been known about since the early 1900's, would there be an organisation dedicated to this research and therefore treating it as a priority?"

"Of that, you can be absolutely certain."

"So it's also possible someone has already worked it out."

"The theory of time travel, when Albert Einstein wrote his theory of relativity, theorised that space and time are intimately linked. In 1916, Einstein wrote his general theory of relativity, which showed that space and time are malleable. Essentially, they respond to the presence of matter or energy by warping, bending, expanding, and contracting. Imagine space being filled with a negative form of energy. Space and time could warp so that time and space could bend back upon themselves like circles, allowing someone to move forward in a straight line and still return to their same starting point in both space and time."

"Have you attempted to disprove his theory?"

"Ahh, well, that takes us back to being unable to produce sufficient exotic matter in time for it to work.

There's another issue with time travel, and that is, if we travelled back in time to change an event, it would create a ripple effect, effectively changing what's taking place right now, between you and I in this very moment. You could travel back in time to ensure the time machine itself was never invented, thus negating everything as the change itself prevents this event from happening in the first place.

To elaborate, I could hop into a time machine, use it to go back in time for 5 minutes and destroy the very same time machine. If I destroy it, it would be impossible for me to use it 5 minutes later.

And so what we believe is that with that magnitude of power, you would change the course of history and the world, each event resulting in a potentially different outcome for the world but never repeatable.

However, what it actually means in principle is paradoxical because if I cannot use the time machine, then I cannot go back in time and destroy it. It cannot be both destroyed and not destroyed simultaneously."

"What if they agreed that anyone travelling back in time is only permitted to observe rather than make any significant changes, as you suggest?"

"Well, yes, one would hope there would be guidelines, however, we are relying on heavily restricting who can and cannot travel and limiting is not something synonymous with explorers and inventors."

"But it's likely anyone who found a way to build a time machine wouldn't divulge the fact to the public."

"Correct. In the wrong hands, it would be a catastrophe."

"If anyone has invented a time machine, Mr. Collings, that would be the catastrophe."

"Quite right, my dear. Now, if that will be all, I really must be on my way. Take heed, young lady; those looking to hide truths will do anything to ensure they remain hidden."

Eleanor felt the chill in his warning. She didn't have a choice; knowledge of a sinister, secret organisation with the potential to manipulate time in some manner couldn't be ignored.

Her research intensified, and she began creating a map, noting the complex web of seemingly unrelated events in her town. Next, she began writing down all she knew – the increase in suicides, the negativity, the apathy, the series of awful events which felt...conspired. The strange adverts and the unusual social media posts meant the potential for major corporations to be subtly involved, their products potentially laden with something, their marketing campaigns designed to sow discord and unhappiness. Media was resolutely silent, and this, to Eleanor, confirmed their involvement.

Government agencies were clearly complicit, their intelligence services actively suppressing any hint of the truth, or the events wouldn't have led to this point. The cabal's reach, it appeared, extended into every facet of modern society.

Eleanor had a thought: what if the negative energy was somehow being harnessed? Could it really be possible this cabal was using the collective negative energy generated by the widespread despair and suicides to fuel a dangerous, highly unstable time-travel experiment? Human misery, their suffering, was the fuel powering their insane ambition?

Her hands trembled as her eyes scanned her notes. The map linking everything together, pointed to the truth. The cold dread of realisation crept into her bones. This was beyond anything she could have conceived. It explained everything: the meticulously planned misfortunes taking place over decades, drawn out and purposeful, the subtle manipulation of the media and social networks, the unsettling behaviour of those around her. It was a coordinated assault on the human spirit, a grand scheme of control fuelled by the darkest aspects of human experience. But what type of humans were doing this? Who was this Synarchy?

She looked at the sleeping form of Warrick beside her, his breathing slow and even. He remained blissfully unaware of the horrifying truth she now possessed. Telling him, she knew, would be a challenge. He was a man of logic, of reason, and this reality, as absurd and terrifying as it was, was a bridge too far for his sceptical mind. The thought of trying to explain it to him filled her with a mixture of fear and dreaded determination.

Warrick had taken to retreating into the mundane, his method of coping with the sheer absurdity of their situation. Or perhaps it was the nano-tech controlling his mind.

The next morning, whilst making breakfast, she confronted him.

"Warrick," Eleanor began, her voice tight with a weary frustration she couldn't quite conceal, "Did you see this article on the sudden spike in suicides among middle-aged men? The ones that seem almost... planned? The exact demographic we fit into...."

He grunted non-committally, his eyes glued to his phone, watching a funny video on some social platform. A canned laugh echoed from the screen, a jarring counterpoint to the icy dread that had settled in Eleanor's heart.

"Eleanor," Warrick said, finally tearing his gaze away, "It's a coincidence. People are dealing with a lot of stress right now, and yes, it is unfortunate, but it seems fairly normal suicides are on the increase during a time of crisis. As for us, we're just having a run of bad luck. We've been hit hard, I know, but this... conspiracy thing? You're sounding like your friend Penelope." He chuckled. "You're letting the stress get to you. You need a holiday. A long one."

"A holiday?" Eleanor echoed, a bitter laugh escaping her lips. "We're living in a Kafkaesque nightmare, Warrick! Our lives are being systematically destroyed by some unseen puppet master, and you want a holiday?"

He sighed, rubbing his temples. "Look, Eleanor, I get it.

Losing our jobs, barely clinging onto the house... it's all been a brutal blow. But this... this talk of nano-tech controlling our minds, people orchestrating our downfall... it's just... far-fetched." He gave a dismissive wave of his hand. "Even for the ridiculously bleak state of our lives right now."

Eleanor's patience, already frayed to the breaking point, snapped. "Far-fetched? Warrick, the evidence is overwhelming! The patterns, the timing, the sheer scale of it all – it's not coincidence! It's all linked!" She paced the room, her voice rising with each step. "Remember Dr. Albright's presentation on microscopic particles and behavioural modification?

Remember how he dismissed the research? And how he mysteriously died a week later? Remember the suspicious 'accidental' lab fire that erased all his research?"

Warrick shook his head. He offered a counterpoint that was less logical deduction and more a desperate attempt to cling to normalcy. "Alright, let's assume, for the sake of argument, that there is some kind of shadowy organisation out there messing with our lives. Why us? Why not some CEO or a politician? Why a relatively average couple living in a quiet town?"

"Maybe," Eleanor argued, "because we represent something to them. Something they can't control. Our love? It might be the unexpected variable."

Warrick chuckled again, this time a touch less strained. "Our love? Seriously, Eleanor? Do you really think some clandestine cabal, as you put it, is actively trying to sabotage our marriage?"

He paused, then added, with a hint of dark humour, "If that's their goal, they're doing a piss-poor job. Now hurry on back upstairs, darling...if you know what I mean?" he said with a wink.

Eleanor sighed and leaned against the wall, running a hand through her tangled hair. Warrick's awareness had not only done a complete u-turn but he was showing signs of something else.

She felt very afraid and alone, and her voice began shakily "Warrick, they've been actively trying to destroy us for decades." She knew their love for each other was the one thing that felt real and tangible in this surreal, increasingly horrifying reality. And she knew he'd been compromised by the god-awful nano-tech.

She started again, choosing a different tack, a softer approach. "Warrick, what if I told you that this strong sense of intuition that I have about this isn't just a flight of fancy? It's as though I'm being propelled by something far greater than myself, and I cannot, despite all the best will in the world, ignore all of this that I'm witnessing....I'm also feeling things, some kind of energy...I don't know what this is, but I'm seeing things."

Warrick raised an eyebrow, "Seriously?" He let out a low whistle. "Okay, now you're really going mad."

"No, listen," Eleanor pleaded, "I've found more evidence. I'm in the process of compiling it all."

They stared at each other for a brief moment and noticing his wife's expression was one of concern, Warrick softened.

"Okay, show me what you have when you've compiled it all, and I'll take a look."

A small, hesitant smile played on Eleanor's lips. A crack in Warrick's wall of cynicism had appeared, a tiny fissure in his stubborn disbelief. It was a beginning. A fragile, tentative start in a fight against overwhelming odds. But it was a start, and in this nightmare they were living, it ignited a spark of hope within. The fight for survival against an unseen enemy was becoming intertwined with a fight for the survival of their relationship and the steadfast refusal to accept the absurd reality they found themselves inhabiting.

Crossing Paths

The rain hammered against the corrugated iron roof of the shed, a relentless percussion accompanying the frantic beating of Eleanor's heart. The air hung thick with the smell of damp earth and a citrusy smell similar to sweet orange. She'd followed the cryptic instructions scrawled on the back of a faded postcard – a postcard she'd found inexplicably tucked inside Winston's favourite squeaky toy, a rather unsettling discovery in itself.

The message, written by an unsteady hand, had simply read: "Seek shelter where the green signs paths cross, and willows weep, 500 yards towards the greatest blue, the dusty path to the future on the left, and there lies the hidden place you seek. The truth awaits."

With her acutely tuned mind, it didn't take her much time to decrypt the message. She'd known the green signs referenced the old quarry, and great blue could only mean the ocean. There was a hidden secluded beach only reachable by foot, and she knew the path and would follow it.

She found the large shed nestled deep within a copse of ancient willows, their branches majestically bowed. Inside, huddled beneath a thick woollen blanket, sat a woman who looked as weathered and ancient as the trees themselves. Her face, etched with the map of a life lived hard, was framed by a halo of silver hair that seemed to shimmer in the weak light filtering through the gaps in the corrugated iron.

"You're Eleanor?" the woman said, her voice soothing like the soft rustling of willow leaves in the wind.

Eleanor nodded her throat tight with a mixture of apprehension and morbid curiosity. She'd spent the last few weeks navigating a world that had become increasingly surreal, a landscape populated by people whose behaviour shifted like sand dunes in a gale. The initial dismissals –"stress," "a touch of the sun," "middle-age melancholy" – had crumbled like biscuit crumbs under the weight of escalating strangeness. Now, she found herself in a crumbling shed, about to meet someone who apparently held the key to the madness unfolding around her.

"They call me Agnes," the woman continued, her gaze unwavering. "And I know more than you can imagine about what's been happening in this blessed little corner of the world."

Agnes's story unfolded slowly, a tapestry woven from threads of ancient folklore and cutting- edge technology. It began, she explained, centuries ago, with a clandestine Synarchy dedicated to harnessing energies from the ley lines that crisscrossed the verdant countryside. These were not your average new-age hippy ley lines; although yet to be scientifically explained, these are powerful currents of raw energy being harnessed for nefarious purposes. The Synarchy, she revealed, had been quietly accumulating power for generations, its members hidden within our society, their influence insidious and far-reaching.

"But it's not just ancient magic," Agnes explained, her voice dropping to a conspiratorial whisper. "They've harnessed it, amplified it, using technology that would make you weep. Quantum entanglement, subtle energy manipulation... the sort of thing that keeps most physicists up at night, worrying about the ethical implications."

The rain intensified, the wind howling like a banshee outside. Eleanor, despite her initial weariness, found herself captivated by Agnes's narrative. The woman spoke with an authority that transcended simple storytelling; there was a conviction in her eyes, a grim determination etched into every line of her face.
"The ultimate goal?" Agnes leaned closer, her breath misting in the cold air. "A time-travel machine. A machine powered by despair, specifically suicide."

The words hung in the air, heavy and suffocating. The unsettling words solidifying the conversations she'd had with others, the changes she'd witnessed in her friends and family – the lethargy, the sudden inexplicable sadness, the whispers of self-destruction – it all clicked into place.
Agnes described the machine in chilling detail. It wasn't a clunky, Hollywood-style contraption; it was far more subtle. It fed on negative emotions, on the despair and hopelessness that the Synarchy cultivated through their manipulation. The more despair they generated, the stronger the machine became its potential to rewrite history growing exponentially.
"They're not just altering lives," Agnes spoke, her voice laced with bitter resentment. "They're rewriting the history of time itself."
She described the Synarchy's methods: subtle psychological manipulations, targeted disinformation campaigns, and the

strategic deployment of fear and uncertainty. They were masters of manipulation, weaving their influence through the everyday lives of ordinary people, subtly altering perceptions, influencing decisions, and driving individuals towards despair. It was a chillingly effective strategy, Agnes explained, and it was working with terrifying efficiency.

"They use technology to amplify their ancient magic," Agnes continued, her voice low. "Subtle energy waves, imperceptible to most, but capable of altering brain chemistry, triggering specific emotions, planting suggestions. They've been working on this for centuries, perfecting their craft, building their machine."

Eleanor's mind raced, trying to reconcile the fantastical elements of Agnes's story with the unnerving reality of her own experiences. The seemingly insignificant events – the hushed conversations, missing people and belongings, everyone's unusual behaviour, including Winston's – now seemed less like random occurrences and more like carefully arranged pieces in a larger, more terrifying puzzle.

The shed creaked ominously, and the wind howled again, rattling the windows. The rain, it seemed, was mirroring Eleanor's inner turmoil. She was now firmly planted in a world of clandestine meetings, whispers in the dark, and the terrifying possibility of time-travel manipulation.

"But why?" Eleanor asked, her voice barely a whisper. "Why would they do all this?"

Agnes sighed a long, weary sound. "Power, Eleanor. Control. They believe they can reshape the world according to their own twisted vision, a vision free from what they deem imperfections."

"We cannot allow this. We need to do something...but what, where do we even begin?" Eleanor asked, her voice trembling slightly. Deep down, she knew that she couldn't simply ignore this, walk away, and pretend it wasn't happening. The changes in her friends and family were too real, too disturbing.

Agnes looked at her, a glint of something akin to hope flickering in her eyes. "You're stronger than you think, Eleanor. You've already seen more than most. Now, you must decide if you're willing to fight."

The weight of Agnes' words "willing to fight" pressed down on Eleanor, the enormity of the task before her almost crushing. But as she looked at Agnes, at the steely determination in her gaze, a spark of defiance ignited within her. She might be a middle-aged woman with a fondness for high-quality loose-leaf tea and a simple life, but she wasn't about to let some shadowy organisation manipulate her, nor anyone she cared about. This wasn't just about saving her family and friends, however; it was about saving time itself. The rain outside continued to fall, but now, it felt less like a mournful lament and more like a battle cry.

Ancient Energies and Modern Tech

The afternoon was drawing in, and Agnes, her face illuminated by the flickering beam of an old lamp and candles, traced a finger across a complex diagram etched into the cold concrete floor. It resembled a circuit board with symbols that looked like ancient lines and diagrams intertwined with modern circuitry. The air, still thick with that organic tang, crackled with a low hum that vibrated in Eleanor's throat.

"This drawing," Agnes whispered, her voice barely audible above the drumming rain, "is a replica of the heart of their operation. The nexus, if you will."
Eleanor peered closer, her breath fogging in the cool air. The diagram showed a series of interconnected nodes marked with a different symbol. Some resembled Celtic knots, others Egyptian hieroglyphs, and still others were undeniably modern technological representations – transistors, microchips, and a complex energy source schematic.

"Ancient energies... harnessed by modern technology," Agnes continued, her voice laced with a chilling blend of awe and revulsion. "They've found a way to amplify and manipulate these energies, to... to weaponise them."

"They've tapped into prominent ley lines, Eleanor. Those energetic pathways that run beneath the earth have been used for centuries, but now, with their advanced technology, they've amplified their power exponentially."

Eleanor had heard whispers of ley lines, of ancient energy currents coursing through the earth, but had always dismissed them as folklore. Now, facing the undeniable evidence before her – the intricate diagram, the humming energy – she felt a shiver of genuine fear.

"And the technology?" Eleanor prompted. "What kind of technology are we talking about?"

Agnes sighed, running a hand through her already dishevelled silver hair. "Think of the most advanced technology you can imagine – quantum computing, bioengineering, even… time manipulation. They've pushed the boundaries of what's possible, combining ancient knowledge with cutting-edge science. It's… unholy."

"Time manipulation?" Eleanor gasped, the word hanging heavy in the air. The postcard, the cryptic message, the urgency of Agnes's warnings – it all pointed to something unseemly.

"Yes," Agnes confirmed grimly. "They've built a machine. A time-travel machine powered by this… this unholy fusion of ancient energies and modern tech. It's feeding on despair, on the suffering they inflict. Each act of despair fuels its power, with each suicide propelling it exponentially, strengthening its power."

It was a scenario straight out of a dystopian novel, yet here she was, in a damp shed in the idyllic countryside, staring at the evidence of its terrifying reality.

"They use a combination of subtle psychological manipulation and direct technological intervention," Agnes explained, her voice taking on a more analytical tone. "The ancient energies amplify. They intensify emotions, making people more susceptible to negative suggestions. The technology then provides the precision tools for targeted manipulation."

She pointed to a specific symbol on the diagram resembling a coiled serpent. "That symbol," she said, "represents a particular ley line that runs just outside this very town. They've tapped into it, using sophisticated arrays of concealed antennae on the outskirts of town. These antennae emit a low-frequency signal, barely perceptible to the human ear, but it subtly alters brainwave patterns, making people more prone to negativity, hopelessness, and ultimately, suicide."

Eleanor struggled to reconcile this explanation with her previous perceptions. She'd dismissed the strange behaviour of her friends and neighbours as stress, exhaustion, and even the onset of mid-life crises. Now, she realised the chilling truth: they had been victims of a meticulously planned, technologically advanced manipulation campaign.

Agnes continued, explaining the intricate workings of the Synarchy's technology. "They're likely to be using advanced AI to analyse vast quantities of data – social media posts, news articles, even overheard conversations – to identify individuals who are vulnerable to their manipulation. They then tailor their messaging and signals to target specific individuals, pushing them towards despair and self-destruction."

"But how can they control people so effectively?" Eleanor asked, her mind reeling from the information overload.

"The network of individuals involved is staggering. They have people in all walks of life, all sectors. When people are already down, they're far easier to manipulate to all-out depression and suicide." Agnes clarified. "It's about nudges, manipulations that exploit existing vulnerabilities. They're not zapping people with mind control rays; they're whispering suggestions into their subconscious minds, already fragile from their nefarious sabotage, then using those dark energies, they amplify their negative thoughts and emotions, pushing them towards a predetermined outcome."

She pointed to another symbol, a stylized image of a human brain intersected by a series of lines that resembled laser beams. "That's their representation of the targeted neurological manipulation. They're using focused bursts of energy, precisely calibrated to specific brain regions, to influence mood, behaviour, even decision-making."

The sheer sophistication of the Synarchy's methods stunned Eleanor. It wasn't brute force but surgical precision, a blend of ancient mysticism and advanced technology working in horrifying synergy.
Agnes's expression grew even more serious. "The machine requires a tremendous amount of energy. That's where the multitude of despair, the suicides, come in. Each act of self-destruction generates a surge of negative energy that is channelled into the machine, storing it for their twisted time travel."

The rain outside had begun to subside, the organic scent in the air lessening as the storm moved on. But the storm inside Eleanor raged on, a tempest of fear, anger, and determination. She looked at Agnes, at the steely resolve in her eyes, and felt a surge of grim satisfaction. She wasn't alone in this fight. She had an ally, a powerful and knowledgeable ally, and together, they would confront the Synarchy and its unholy alliance of ancient energies and modern technology. The fight for time itself had begun, and she was ready.

The Time Travel Machine

Agnes tapped her screen to reveal a drawing, the one that resembled a stylized serpent. The air grew colder. A chill seeped into Eleanor's bones despite her thick wool coat. The symbols pulsed faintly, their glow a sickly green that mirrored the unnatural hue of a city in some dystopian futuristic film.

"This," Agnes said, her voice hushed, "is the heart of it. The machine."

Eleanor stared at the diagram and the intricate lines and circuitry network. It was beautiful in a horrifying, alien way, a testament to both ancient wisdom and terrifying technological prowess. The vileness of it all - to harness despair and suicide to power a time-travel machine - left her speechless.

"How did they work out how to build this, to do all of this?" Eleanor finally managed to croak out, her voice trembling slightly.

Agnes sighed. "The Synarchy... they're using ancient energies to guide them, is my belief, the energies have led them to discoveries such as the connection between human emotion – specifically, the overwhelming despair of hopelessness, the finality of suicide – and the temporal currents of reality itself. The technical side, perhaps driven by modern technology, but the ability to build a time machine has always been a desire of theirs, and with their money, power and influence, it would appear they forged through with it."

Eleanor felt a wave of nausea wash over her. The sheer depravity of it was staggering. They weren't just manipulating people; they were actively *harvesting* their despair, their pain, and their very deaths to fuel their infernal machine.

"And the suicides... they're definitely suicides then, they're not accidental deaths as has been reported?" Eleanor whispered, the question hanging heavy in the air.

Agnes nodded grimly. "Far from it. They're carefully orchestrated. The Synarchy uses a combination of subtle psychological manipulation, advanced neuro-linguistic programming, and...well, let's just say they have certain...persuasive techniques." She paused, her gaze fixed on the diagram. "They target potential dissenters, anyone who can see through the facade and question, anyone with special gifts such as high intelligence and empathy, the vulnerable, the lonely, those who feel lost and alone. They whisper promises of escape, of oblivion, and then... they deliver. They infiltrate local councils, charities, and even schools. They spread misinformation, subtly undermine confidence, and foster division. It's all part of a grand strategy to break the human spirit, to create the perfect breeding ground for their...harvest."

The image of her friends and family, their smiles replaced by vacant stares, their vibrant lives extinguished by the insidious touch of the Synarchy, filled her mind. The thought was unbearable.

"But why?" Eleanor asked, her voice laced with a desperate plea for understanding. "Why would they want to control time?"

Agnes looked up, her eyes filled with a mixture of sorrow and grim determination. "Control, Eleanor, is the ultimate power.

Imagine the possibilities: rewriting history, eliminating rivals, securing their power for eternity. They believe they are destined to rule, not just this world, but all of them."

Eleanor, with trepidation, her voice trembling with a mixture of fear and resolve.
"So, what can we do?"

Agnes straightened up, a flicker of something akin to hope in her eyes. "We need to understand exactly how this machine works, how to disable it. We need to know how many machines there are. To do that, we need to delve deeper into the Synarchy's history and uncover its secrets. Their hidden agendas. We need to find their weaknesses and exploit them."

Agnes pointed to a specific diagram, a complex symbol that resembled a twisted key. "This one," she explained, "I believe is the key to understanding the machine's power source. It's a potential conduit, drawing the negative energy from the suicides and channelling it into the temporal distortion field."
"And how do we stop it?" Eleanor asked her voice tight with urgency.
"We disrupt the flow," Agnes replied, her voice low and intense. "We sever the connection between the despair and the machine. We starve the beast, is my opinion, but we need more research and we need more research and more time." She paused, a thoughtful expression on her face. "And that's easier said than done. The Synarchy has layers of protection and intricate safeguards. We need a plan, a precise, meticulously crafted plan."

As the afternoon turned to evening, it carried a blur of activity. Agnes, with her limited knowledge of ancient lore and surprisingly adept technological skills, explained her understanding of the workings of the machine in more detail.

Eleanor, despite her initial shock and disbelief, found a strange sort of focus, a grim determination that fuelled her through the complexity of the situation.

They discovered the machine wasn't just a single device; it was a network, a complex system of interconnected nodes scattered across the country, each drawing on the collective despair of those who had fallen victim to the Synarchy's manipulations. They were like parasitic tendrils, sucking the lifeblood out of society, feeding the monstrous machine that threatened to destroy the history of humanity.

Agnes produced a series of maps, meticulously drawn and annotated with cryptic symbols. Each map depicted a location – a seemingly innocuous building, a forgotten garage, an abandoned house – where it was possible a node of the machine was located. The maps were not just geographical but also temporal, indicating periods when the nodes were most vulnerable to attack.

"We need to strike at each node simultaneously," Agnes explained, pointing to a cluster of locations on one of the maps. "Disable them one by one, disrupting the flow of negative energy. It's a race against time, Eleanor. If we don't succeed, the Synarchy will achieve their ultimate goal." The weight of the responsibility pressed down on her, heavy and suffocating. The fate of the future she knew, rested on her shoulders.

"How do we do it?" Eleanor asked, her voice barely a whisper. The task seemed insurmountable, a Herculean effort beyond her capabilities.

Agnes smiled, a rare and genuine smile that radiated warmth and strength. "We use their own weapons against them, Eleanor. We exploit their weaknesses. We use their technology against them." She revealed a small, intricately designed device on her computer, a size no bigger than a matchbox. "This," she said, "is a frequency disruptor. It can overload the nodes, temporarily shutting them down. But we need to be precise, fast, and extremely careful. I have people working on the build of it."

Eleanor stared at the diagram of the device, a small spark of hope flickering in her heart.

The Scope of the Conspiracy

The air in the shed hung thick with the smell of old paper and a smokey leather jacket. Agnes traced a finger across a complex diagram drawn on a faded map. It depicted a network of lines snaking across Britain, connecting seemingly innocuous locations – a crumbling manor house, a disused railway station, and a seemingly ordinary bookshop. Each point, Agnes explained, represented a pointer of Synarchy influence.

"It's far bigger than we thought," Agnes said, her voice low and serious. "This isn't just about manipulating individuals. They're controlling entire communities, entire swathes of the population. Look at this," she tapped a point near the coastline. "This is where I believe they harvest the... the essence."

Eleanor shivered, the chilling cold that had clung to the air lingered. The "essence," Agnes had explained, was a vital component in their infernal machine – a dark energy drawn from the despair and hopelessness of their victims.

The more despair they cultivated, the more powerful the machine became.

She pointed to another cluster of points, this time concentrated around The City. "See these? These are their major communication hubs. They use a combination of advanced technology and... older methods. Think subtle mind control, Eleanor. Not outright zombies, but individuals subtly nudged towards self-destruction."

The map was a chilling insight into the Synarchy's pervasive influence. Agnes had previously explained how they used targeted advertising, manipulation of social media, and seemingly benign community initiatives to cultivate a sense of moroseness and hopelessness, feeding the time-travel machine with the essence of human suffering.

"How could anyone be so... evil?" Eleanor asked, her voice tinged with disbelief. The thought of individuals systematically orchestrating the destruction of lives on such a vast scale was almost incomprehensible.

"Some are true believers," Agnes replied, her eyes filled with a sorrowful understanding. "Others are simply power-hungry, blinded by ambition and the promise of unimaginable power. Many are simply unwitting pawns caught in their insidious web. And some," she paused, her gaze distant, "are tragically broken people, manipulated and used for their vulnerability."

"I need to tell you, I met a woman called Seraphina. She found me, I don't know how, but she claims to be the daughter of one of the higher-ups in The Synarchy. She said she wants to help. She hasn't provided any further input other than what you have said today. She could be a really good ally."

"Or an incredibly evil foe." chimed Agnes. "I would need more information about her, but let's come back to that later. Thank you for telling me."

"There's something else. I wasn't sure whether to mention it but given all you've shared, it might be relevant. I found this silver box. It has an emblem engraved, and, well, actually, my dog, Winston, dug it up. There's...an energy emitted from it, and I believe it belongs to this Synarchy." Eleanor said.

Agnes stared at her for a few moments and then said, "Do you have it with you? Can I see it?"

Eleanor pulled it out of her bag. "I think the symbol relates to the old energies and has some sort of power, but I don't really understand how," she said.

"It's evil. We need to get rid of it properly, and never allow anyone to know you had it. If you find anything else similar to this, bring it here, and I will destroy it."

"How can energy be trapped inside a box? I felt its vibration, its pull, and I've never experienced anything like that before in my life."

"The Synarchy has found a way to trap energy, this appears to be one of their first prototypes." Agnes delivered with a soft, monotone voice.

"There's a hidden Synarchy meeting planned for next week, somewhere in the heart of Chestingbourne." she continued. "A high-level gathering, a meeting where the Synarchy's elite would likely be discussing their plans. It's a risky move, but it is a chance to gather concrete evidence and expose their operations to the world."

"This meeting," Agnes repeated, her voice hardening with purpose. "This is our chance. If we can expose them, even partially, it could destabilise their operation. The sheer scale of it might shatter the foundation of their influence."

"I'd like you to meet the team I've assembled. Tomorrow, you'll meet with them at The Old Spoon pub. I can't get around like you youngsters." Eleanor noted her fragile state and wondered how long Agnes had. Her fierce eyes and fighting spirit betrayed her fragile appearance.

"How did you find me?" Eleanor asked with mild curiosity.
"It was through Wilson he noticed you checking out a number of unconventional books at the library. And he saw something in you, that perhaps you were researching the same subject as we are. He took a chance."

It was nearing nine pm when Eleanor finally left Agnes, the rocky path eerily lit by a small torch Agnes gave her, the chilly silence of the night air, broken by her own footsteps and the intermittent hooting of an owl in the distance. Her fear was palpable.

When she reached her vehicle, she half expected it to be gone, but it was there waiting for her exactly where she left it. When she arrived home, Winston gave her a lovely welcome home wag, and she stroked his belly for a while, his warm, furry belly a striking contrast to the cold chill she felt in her heart. Warrick was sound asleep, and she curled up beside him, warming herself against his back.

"I missed you tonight," she whispered.

A Meeting

The following morning, she made Warrick an omelette for breakfast and kept the conversation as light as she could manage. He informed her about an upcoming interview with a large engineering firm, one he needed to prepare for - a position in the city. A daunting prospect he'd been dreading, up against a high number of candidates in the current climate. He had a few days to prepare for it and was brushing up on new interview techniques and taking Winston for long walks to clear his mind. She told him she'd been visiting friends the night before, which was true. She considered Agnes a solid ally. Warrick thought back to her words the night before, "I missed you tonight." he'd been awake when his wife had climbed into bed, but he'd thought better than to start an argument. They were both under stress. He'd fallen asleep after hearing her words. She missed him - he missed her too.

The location of their meeting was an old pub on the outskirts of town, run by the pub landlord, Mr. Sale. The flickering gaslight created an eerie glow around the back room of "The Old Spoon," a bar that smelled perpetually of stale beer and worn carpets. The old stone walls and dimly lit interior fit the way Eleanor felt: cold and with a sense of foreboding. Eleanor nervously adjusted the worn strap of her messenger bag, its contents – pepper spray, water and a flash drive containing incriminating data – a heavy weight on her shoulders.

Just as despair threatened to engulf her, a flicker of movement caught her eye. From behind a stack of rusty barrels, a figure emerged, silhouetted against the faint light filtering through a grimy window. He wore jeans and a casual shirt, gaunt, his caramel-coloured skin unable to hide his dark, hollow eyes - but there was a spark in his gaze, a flicker of defiance that resonated with Eleanor's own desperate hope. Another figure emerged, then another, until a small group of four stood before her, their faces a mixture of apprehension and determination.

Eleanor glanced down at the diamond-encrusted bracelet she put on each day and pulled her sleeve over to cover it.
"Agnes wanted me to meet you." Eleanor extended her hand.
The first introduced himself as Ralph, and the others followed suit. Each had a story of suffering, of manipulation, of near-breakdowns, of the mental and emotional torture inflicted.
Ralph explained that they had been monitoring the Synarchy's activities for months, gathering intelligence and searching for others who were resistant to the control. They'd met each other on one of the chat forums and it was a leap of faith arranging to meet in person.
"You're different to what I expected," Ralph continued, his voice hushed with reverence.
"I'm here to help any way I can." with her hand, she gestured for everyone to sit. "Shall we talk?"
A short, wiry man named Trevor, his eyes darting nervously; a tall, sturdy man named Ivor, his arms crossed defensively; and a surprisingly sharp-eyed-looking older gentleman named Wilson, who was calmly sipping a glass of what Eleanor suspected was orange juice.

They were an unlikely group, united only by a shared suspicion – a suspicion that gnawed at their sanity, a suspicion that whispered of a conspiracy so vast, so insidious, it threatened to consume the world.

"It started subtly," Ralph began, his voice a low tremor.

"Increased anxiety, insomnia, a feeling of... disconnect. I lost my job, my apartment, and my girlfriend all within six months. I was a mess, a walking, talking zombie. Then I started noticing patterns, connections, things that didn't add up." He scratched his leg intensely. "And the worst part? Not one person in my life would listen to what I was saying – not one."

Trevor nodded grimly, his expression mirroring Ralph's despair. "My family... they're gone. Not dead, exactly, but...changed. They're distant, apathetic. Like puppets with their strings cut, just going through the motions. I tried to help them, to reach them, but... it's like they're not even there anymore." He looked at Eleanor, his eyes filled with an empty sadness. "I've lost everything," he rubbed his brow, "just too shocked to grieve."

Wilson chuckled dryly. "Well, I lost my prize-winning petunias." He took a long sip of his drink. "Absolutely magnificent specimens. Vanished, without a trace. It was odd. No signs of disease, no pests... just... pulled out from the ground, never to be seen again." A flicker of something darker – fear, perhaps – momentarily crossed his face before he resumed his jovial façade. "Those and my family. Son to suicide and wife to gleeful apathy if there is such a thing."

"I lost everything, literally, everything. I'm currently couch surfing, but I've no idea where I'll be sleeping tonight. I live day by day, hour by hour and well, these chaps have been my lifeline. I'm Ivor, by the way, with a strong northern accent. My occupation was security, head of IT security for a large firm. I was on six figures, to give you some idea of the lifestyle that I had. And now I'm sitting in a dive bar, a place I'd have avoided in my previous life."

Eleanor felt a wave of empathy wash over her. Their stories, each one unique, painted a chilling picture of a world slowly succumbing to a silent, invisible enemy. The shared experiences, however, confirmed her own suspicions, strengthening her resolve. She couldn't stand alone anymore. She needed allies, a strong force of resistance.

"I've got something that might help," Eleanor said. She reached into her bag and produced the flash drive. "It contains data that I've collated, some of it we might find useful."

They all exchanged glances, their expressions a mixture of hope and apprehension.

They spent the next few hours huddled around a laptop, poring over their shared documents, images, and recordings. The evidence was being uncovered, and the level of depravity chilled Eleanor to the bone. The Synarchy's desire for power and control wasn't simply about manipulating individuals; it wasn't simply about controlling entire systems –governments, corporations, media outlets, their true goal: time travel, not for altruistic purposes, but self-preservation. They were using the despair and negativity generated by energies to power a temporal device, a means to escape the impending consequences of their actions.

As the night deepened, a sense of grim determination settled upon the group. They were fighting for the future of humanity. The sheer scale of the conspiracy was daunting, but the shared knowledge and the unexpected camaraderie fuelled a newfound strength. This small, unlikely alliance represented a flicker of hope in a world descending into darkness.

Ivor, his eyes narrowing as he sipped his coffee, scanning Trevor's laptop screen, "You know, if you're leaving this many open ports, you're basically inviting a hacker to a party. And trust me, they're RSVP-ing."
Trevor, tapping the keyboard enthusiastically, "Oh, I've got something far better on this little machine - I use a VPN. It's completely untraceable."
"Good lad," Ivor responded.

Their combined intelligence revealed that the cabal wasn't simply controlling minds; they were harnessing the negative energy generated by despair and suffering to power their time-travel experiments. The more people succumbed to despair, the stronger their time-travel machine became.
The cabal's goal, it seemed, was not just to dominate humanity but to reshape history, to rewrite the past to their own nefarious designs. The implications were staggering, a horror that threatened to unravel the very foundations of reality.

Trevor, a tech expert, would use his skills to record the proceedings, whilst Ivor, due to his large size and tech skills, would provide both security and tactical support. Ralph was their driver, although ordinarily he was an informed scientific researcher and Wilson, a highly intellectual history scholar whose knowledge bordered the esoteric, was instrumental in understanding and interpreting their methodology.
With her intuition and innate ability to connect with people and understand their motivations, Eleanor would act as a liaison,

seeking to identify key vulnerabilities within the Synarchy's structure.

Ivor handed Eleanor what appeared to be a large mobile phone, "Before we go, here is a secure burner phone...you will need this when communicating with all of us. Our numbers are programmed into the phone, and it works just like a normal phone with a few quirks." he pressed a few buttons on the handset to show her how to use it. "It cannot be tracked nor traced by anyone, including the Synarchy, so you have nothing to fear."

"Thank you, thank you all so much...for everything, you have no idea..." Eleanor's voice trailed off.

"We're just as pleased to meet you, Eleanor," Trevor said and smiled reassuringly.

Heating up

The next few days were a whirlwind of frantic activity.

Ralph, Trevor and Ivor painstakingly crafted a miniature surveillance device, small enough to be concealed easily, capable of recording audio and video footage with exceptional clarity.

Eleanor meticulously planned their infiltration route, identified potential escape routes, and devised a series of cryptic codes they could use to communicate discretely during the operation. Wilson would be looking out for anything historic, artefacts, anything to be used as evidence and Winston, the dog, would be a perfect cover.

The infiltration was a seamless mixture of stealth and cunning. The meeting took place in a secluded lakeside cottage, seemingly innocuous but secretly equipped with state-of-the-art surveillance technology. Using her network of contacts, Agnes secured their entry as 'maintenance personnel', a guise that allowed them to blend in without arousing suspicion.

The meeting itself was a chilling spectacle. The Synarchy members, dressed in impeccably tailored suits, spoke in hushed tones, their words veiled in coded language. Trevor's device captured everything, the chilling details of their plans hidden in coded words which Wilson could decode, their callous disregard for human life. Eleanor, observing from the shadows, noted their cold detachment, their unnerving calm amidst the horrifying nature of their discussions. With a sickening certainty, she realised just how deeply entrenched the Synarchy's influence was within society. The scope was beyond their present understanding. They weren't just controlling people. They were shaping their very thoughts, twisting their emotions, exploiting their vulnerabilities to achieve their sinister goals.

The evidence was damning. The recordings revealed not just the existence of the time-travel machine; the nodes they'd previously thought were relevant were not simple energy sources but potentially additional, smaller time machines in their own right, and their initial thoughts had just been reshaped. The Synarchy's ambitious plans were to rewrite history and reshape the world in their own warped image. They were manipulating events on a huge scale, using advanced technology and subtle psychological manipulation to achieve their aims. Their power extended far beyond the quiet countryside; it reached the highest echelons of government, corporate power, and international finance.

As the meeting drew to a close, a tense moment arose. One of the Synarchy members, a man with a glacial stare, seemed to sense their presence. A silent confrontation ensued. With his years of experience in negotiations and knowledge of the Synarchy, Wilson defused the situation with a mixture of charm and a surprisingly effective distraction involving Winston and getting him to pounce onto the buffet table, making it seem an unfortunate accident with a dog misbehaving.

The initial shocks on the faces turned to mild amusement as the "team" dressed in overalls apologised profusely about their dog, Wilson articulating that the dog had recently had an operation and was brain-damaged and deaf. The Synarchy leader's expressions didn't hide their lack of care about the dog's problems. The team made their escape without arousing further scrutiny. Their lives were under direct threat and they were acutely aware of their narrow escape, a frantic dash through the dark, misty countryside, punctuated by the frantic barking of Winston, adding to the intensity.

Back at Agnes' house, reviewing the recording, the weight of their discovery pressed heavily upon them. As they listened to a woman's voice on the recording, "The machines are nearing their final stages....the data looks amazing with the testing in Greenpool and The Capital...." their own voices were quietened. The Synarchy had revealed on tape their sinister plans. The scale of the Synarchy's operation was staggering, their influence extensive and pervasive. The information they had gathered was not just crucial; it was explosive, and the implications were terrifying.

Wilson spoke in a thoughtful tone, holding a mug of tea, "You know, every empire thinks it's different. They think they have the answer - tighter control better systems. The Byzantines, Romans, and Ottomans - all had the same idea. And guess what? They all fell. You see, the rise and fall of civilizations - whether it be the Romans or the Egyptians - has always been about balance. A society grows, reaches its peak, and inevitably begins to unravel when it loses sight of its foundations, the leadership destabilising under the weight of its untenable greed. Absolute power corrupts absolutely..."

Agnes nodded, smiling warmly. "And yet, history repeats itself. Why do you think we haven't learned those lessons?"

"Ah, well. Perhaps we never really learn history. We only think we do until we're faced with new challenges that look far too much like the old ones. The difference now? We have access to more information but less wisdom, perhaps." Wilson gazed out of the window.

Agnes replied, "I happen to agree with you, Wilson. I can't help but wonder if this age will be remembered as one where we understood too little."

Wilson, his eyes weary, "This group of individuals are playing a long game. They've been at this for centuries. If we don't understand what they're doing in the context of history, we'll never understand how to stop them.

They aren't just manipulating the present. They are rewriting history itself, erasing inconvenient truths and manipulating the narrative of the past to justify their grip on power."

Ralph let out a long sigh. "If only we could redirect their ambitions into something constructive instead of this relentless pursuit of dominion. It's as though they believe themselves to be the "architects of all time" but fail to appreciate the weight of that ambition and the responsibility of the repercussions - those who seek power rarely appreciate its weight and, as history has taught us, are crushed before the final act."

Their shared reality, it seemed, was on the precipice of a profound and devastating change.

Alliance

The silence in their cottage felt oppressive, broken only by the rhythmic tick-tock of the grandfather clock in the hall, a sound that now mocked Eleanor with its relentless march of time. Each tick was a hammer blow against her already frayed nerves.

Warrick knew nothing of her meeting with Agnes, nothing of the current situation she was faced with because she didn't believe he'd be able to cope, given his current fragile mental state. Her silence wasn't deceit; it was protection, and she'd need to break it to him gently. She stared out the window, the early morning sun casting a threatening glow across their meticulously tended garden. The roses, usually a vibrant splash of colour, seemed to droop under the weight of an unseen sorrow. Even the air itself felt heavy, thick with a sense of foreboding she couldn't shake.

She had spent the last hour collating the final pieces, meticulously scrutinising every piece of information, to provide him with the most damning evidence proving the most rational explanation for the escalating financial ruin that had befallen them was not mere coincidences. It was a timeline of job losses, unexpected repairs, mysteriously inflated bills – it was a relentless onslaught. Trying to piece it together in such a way as for him to see it. To finally see the truth.

Warrick, sprawled on the sofa, engrossed in a rerun of some ludicrous sitcom, offered a stark contrast to her simmering unease. His obliviousness, usually a source of amusement, now grated on her nerves. "Warrick," she began, her voice laced with a forced calmness, "remember that flat tyre we had a couple of weeks ago, on the way to The Turnbull restaurant?"

Warrick chuckled, his eyes glued to the television screen. "The one that nearly sent us flying into a ditch? Yeah, it wasn't fun, but there's a lot of pothole-ridden roads around here."
Eleanor sighed. "But it was a brand new tyre, Warrick. The mechanic said there was no apparent cause for the puncture. He suggested interference….sabotage."
Warrick snorted. "Sabotage? Eleanor, you're letting this get to you. We're just having a run of bad luck. It happens." He paused, his eyes finally shifting from the screen to her. "Besides, who would want to sabotage us? We're not exactly high-profile targets."
"This is what I've been saying. Who would want to, which has led me to all these new discoveries," Eleanor replied, her voice rising slightly with trepidation. "It's what I've been trying to tell you. Remember the constant financial setbacks, the repeated recessions every few years….
The bullying experienced at every company that I worked at forced me to leave, which had a huge effect on our finances. On top of all that? We finally managed to start my dream and renovate the property, only for it to take an age to sell it. You lost that brilliant job, and we couldn't afford our mortgage, which nearly ended in bankruptcy. Instead of moving on to the next bigger project, we were forced to buy this cottage, or we would have lost everything.
Then it was a series of setbacks again with me unable to find any suitable employment, no headspace and time to write, another of my passions. Remember the tree I purchased, which was planted well and then died a few weeks later?
Remember that faulty wiring in the kitchen? The one that almost started a fire? And the mysterious cracked roof tiles

caused the ceiling to collapse from the weight of water following a heavy rain, soon after we had our roof re-slated? The constant need to replace all our kitchen whites every year due to faulty products out of warranty? The car never running as it should?..." she waited in eager anticipation for a response. Warrick frowned, a hint of concern finally flickering in his eyes. He ran a hand through his already dishevelled hair. "Those things happen every day to all people, Eleanor. Yes, it's a run of misfortune perhaps….not so much unusual, rather, standard. To say it's all sabotage…you're connecting things which aren't in any way connected."

"It's not just unusual, Warrick. It's a pattern," she insisted, her voice trembling slightly. "A calculated pattern. Think about it. The car, the house, the job losses, even Winston going missing…everything happening one after the other. And the financial problems are making it impossible to even cope with the smallest problems."

Eleanor opened the neatly organised file, a meticulously compiled dossier of bank statements, repair bills, incidents and records that she'd been finalising that morning. She laid it out on the coffee table, the sheer volume of documents a testament to her obsessive research.

"I've been connecting the dots, Warrick," she said, her voice low and urgent. "And the picture isn't pretty. It's like someone is systematically dismantling our lives, piece by piece."

Having initially dismissed Eleanor's theories as the ramblings of a distraught woman, Warrick found himself staring at the same chilling evidence. The detailed reports provided a chilling context to their misfortunes. Financially, they were far worse off, transforming random incidents into calculated moves in a larger game. He looked at Eleanor, the doubt in his eyes replaced by a concern.

Warrick glanced at the file, his eyes widening slightly as he took in the sheer amount of evidence.

Eleanor pressed on, her voice regaining its strength.
"Remember that article I showed you a few weeks ago about nanotechnology?"
Warrick's sceptical expression returned. "The one about the government controlling our minds? Eleanor, come on, that was from a conspiracy website."
"But what if it wasn't?" Eleanor countered, her voice rising with a desperate plea. "What if all this – the job losses, the seemingly unconnected series of unfortunate events for people across the country, the accidental deaths, the disappearances – is linked to it? What if this nano stuff is affecting people's behaviour, pushing them towards despair, driving them to make mistakes, and causing accidents and deaths?"
The scepticism on Warrick's face was palpable, but a seed of doubt, however small, had been planted. He wasn't entirely convinced but could no longer dismiss Eleanor's concerns as mere paranoia. He knew Eleanor. She was prone to flights of fancy, but this seemed different.

Eleanor continued, her voice gaining momentum. "I found something else, Warrick. Something that might explain everything." She pulled out a small, velvet-bound journal from her bag. It was old, its pages brittle with age, the cover worn and faded. "I found this in my mother's attic. It belonged to my grandmother. It's filled with entries describing events eerily similar to what we're experiencing. Accidents, illnesses, financial ruin... all meticulously documented. She wrote about a 'shadowy organisation' that manipulates events from the darkness." she looked at him with suggesting eyes.

Warrick's eyes widened. He took the journal carefully, turning its pages slowly. The archaic script was hard to decipher, but the recurring themes were unmistakable – a sinister network pulling strings from the shadows, causing chaos and suffering to achieve their own nefarious ends. A chill ran down his spine. As absurd as the idea was. He wasn't one to entertain such thoughts, but the more she spoke, the more he began to feel the shadow of doubt creep in. He shook his head, trying to clear it.

This wasn't just a series of unfortunate events but something slightly more sinister.
The comedic relief that had punctuated their conversations until now had vanished, replaced by a grim determination. Still reeling from the shock of the journal's contents, Warrick suddenly noticed a small, almost imperceptible shimmer in the air above Eleanor's head. He squinted, rubbing his eyes to make sure he wasn't hallucinating. The shimmering intensified, and then it was gone as quickly as it appeared.

"Did you... see that?" he asked, his voice barely a whisper.
Eleanor nodded, her eyes wide with fear and a burgeoning understanding. "Yes. I've seen it before. Small bursts of...something. Almost like a heat haze, but... different. I think it's related to all of this."
"I've been seeing it for a few days, thought I should book an eye test. Now, having read this...all of your research, this is very compelling, and I'm struggling to find fault with it despite the improbability of it all. Your grandmother's diary is interesting."

Warrick swallowed, the words hitting him harder than he anticipated. He was supposed to be the logical one, the one who could find solutions. But at this moment, nothing wasn't adding up.

"So what now?" he asked quietly, his mind already racing toward the only solution that felt certain: figuring out how to fix his marriage and life and whether his carefully constructed world was as stable as he'd believed. "Maybe this is just a new kind of problem," he thought, trying to ground himself in the familiar. "I'll fix it. I always manage to find a way to fix things." But the uncertainty of his own role in this new equation troubled him.

"I'm just relieved you finally see it. I need you, Warrick. We need each other."

The implications were staggering. If the nano-tech was influencing their lives in this subtle way if it was creating these strange anomalies, what other effects was it having on them on others? The thought sent a fresh wave of icy dread through him. Their initial grief and fear were now overshadowed by a deeper, more pervasive terror – a realisation that they were trapped in a nightmare far grander than their collective minds could conjure up.

The laughter and lighthearted banter that had once filled their home was replaced by a chilling silence, broken only by the frantic ticking of the grandfather clock, a relentless reminder of the time slipping away, of the terrifying truth that was slowly, relentlessly, revealing itself. The battle for their lives, their love, and their future had become a desperate race against an unseen enemy, a fight against a force that controlled not just their lives but the very foundations of their entire reality.

Eleanor knew the only way forward was through and that resistance from Warrick would prove challenging. They couldn't unlearn what they'd learned.

For Eleanor, getting through to Warwick, the love of her life, was a win. She needed to give him time to come to terms with the enormity of it all.

Stepping in

The rain hammered against the windows of the quaint, if slightly damp, village pub, mirroring the turmoil churning within Eleanor. She'd agreed to meet here, a woman shrouded in as much mystery as the Synarchy itself. Wilson, Ralph, Trevor and Ivor had all described as a "wild card," a phrase that, in Agnes' understated manner, "spoke volumes." Even Agnes had said, her access to information that could shatter the Synarchy's carefully constructed façade was "unusual to say the least, but equally, if she were to betray the small team, could shatter everything."

The pub, "The Crooked Spoon," lived up to its name. Its crooked sign creaked morosely in the wind, a fitting preamble to the meeting. Inside, the air hung thick with the scent of stale beer and damp wool. A crackling fire in the hearth offered little comfort against the chill that seeped from the ancient stone walls. Eleanor nervously adjusted her scarf, her gaze darting around the room, searching for any sign of Seraphina. Winston whimpered softly at her feet, his sensitive nose twitching as if sensing the underlying tension.

Then, she saw her. Seated in a shadowy corner booth, a woman with fiery red hair cascaded down her shoulders like a molten river. Her emerald eyes, sharp and intelligent, met Eleanor's across the room. She exuded an aura of quiet confidence, a stark contrast to the nervous energy that permeated the pub. Her attire was unexpected – a tailored, dark grey suit, a touch too formal for a rural pub, yet impeccably stylish, hinting at a life lived outside the confines of the town. She looked like she'd stepped straight out of a stylish international TV set, a stark contrast to Eleanor's own sensible, if slightly mud-splattered, attire.

Eleanor approached cautiously, her heart hammering a frantic rhythm against her ribs. Feeling her apprehension, Winston let out a low growl, a sound quickly swallowed by the pub's boisterous atmosphere. As she neared the booth, Seraphina offered a small, enigmatic smile.

"Eleanor, I hope you don't mind meeting me here?" Her voice was low and melodious, a subtle counterpoint to her sharp gaze.

"I'd have thought it too in the open for you, but this is fine for me," Eleanor replied, settling into the opposite seat.

Winston remained at her feet, a vigilant guardian.

Seraphina leaned forward, her eyes glinting in the dim light. "Tell me, what have you discovered so far?"

Eleanor hesitated, unsure how much to reveal. The weight of the secret felt heavy on her shoulders, the knowledge of the Synarchy's sinister machinations. She began to recount everything, from her experiences, from the subtle behavioural changes among her friends and family but she deliberately left out pertinent information she'd learned from Agnes and the team.

Seraphina listened intently, occasionally interrupting with insightful questions that revealed a deep understanding of the Synarchy's methods. She seemed to possess an intimate knowledge of the organisation's inner workings, her comments laced with both fascination and disgust. At times, a flicker of sadness crossed her face, a hint of personal tragedy resonating with Eleanor's growing despair.

"My father," Seraphina began, her voice hushed, "was one of the Synarchy's most trusted members. He believed in their cause, in their vision of a 'perfected' future. He was blind to the horrors they committed in pursuit of that vision."

A wave of icy dread washed over Eleanor. The daughter of a high-ranking Synarchy member offering assistance… it was too convenient, too perfect. Doubt gnawed at her. Was this genuine help or a meticulously crafted deception? The possibility that Seraphina was a double agent sent to infiltrate Eleanor's nascent rebellion was chillingly plausible.

Seraphina seemed to sense her apprehension. "I understand your scepticism," she said, her voice softer now, tinged with a vulnerability that surprised Eleanor. "Trust isn't easily earned, especially when dealing with individuals like my father. But I assure you, my intentions are genuine. I've seen the horrors they've unleashed, and I want it to end."

She then revealed details that made Eleanor's heart begin to thump. Details about the Synarchy's recruitment process, the methods they used to manipulate individuals, and the inner workings of their time-travel machine. She spoke of hidden symbols, coded messages, and rituals steeped in ancient lore. The information she provided filled in the gaps in Eleanor's understanding, painting a more complete and terrifying picture of the Synarchy's operations.

Seraphina spoke of her father's meticulous notes, hidden within encrypted files that she'd managed to access. These notes revealed not only the technological aspects of their operation but also the philosophical underpinnings of their terrifying plan. They sought to create a "perfect" society, a utopia built on the ashes of the current world, by rewriting history to their liking. This "perfection" however, came at a horrifying cost, a cost paid in despair, suicide, and the erasure of countless lives.

As Seraphina spoke, Eleanor felt a strange mixture of fear and fascination. The revelation of Seraphina's personal connection to the Synarchy added a profound layer of complexity to the situation. It was no longer simply a battle against a faceless organisation but a struggle against a deeply rooted ideology that had infiltrated families, communities, and even her circle of friends.

The night wore on, the rain outside continuing its relentless assault. Eleanor and Seraphina discussed strategies, weighing risks and opportunities. They considered potential allies, assessed the Synarchy's vulnerabilities, and plotted their next move. The conversation flowed effortlessly, their mutual distrust gradually melting away, replaced by a fragile but growing alliance forged in the crucible of a shared purpose.

By the time they parted ways, it was nearing midnight. The air, however, still hummed with the unspoken question: Could Seraphina be trusted? Only time and their perilous journey ahead would tell.

Double Cross

The following morning, Eleanor woke with a crick in her neck and a profound sense of unease. Warrick seemed to take everything in his stride, starting his day with a jog, followed by searching for a new job. Something he'd said he needed to do to maintain their life, regardless of what was or wasn't happening around them. She agreed, appreciating this would maintain the facade, allowing her to continue their plans to put an end to The Synarchy's nefarious plot.

As her mind wandered to the previous night, the tentative alliance forged with Seraphina felt less solid in the cold light of day. The pub, with its low-hanging beams and the lingering smell of stale ale, had provided a cloak of intimacy, a shared space where secrets could be whispered and trust, however fragile, could bloom. But now, back in the sterile environment of her own home, surrounded by the familiar yet somehow alien comfort of her family, doubt nagged at her.

She'd spoken with a confidence that bordered on arrogance, yet her occasional hesitant pauses and nervous twitches suggested a vulnerability that belied her composed exterior. It was a captivating performance, a carefully constructed persona that Eleanor found herself both drawn to and deeply suspicious of. Agnes had voiced her concerns openly. "She's too good to be true, Eleanor," she'd said, her voice laced with the cautious scepticism that was her trademark. "The daughter of a high-ranking Synarchy member offering help? It's convenient, almost too convenient." She'd reminded her of the many twists and turns they'd already faced, the unexpected betrayals and seemingly impossible alliances. Her words, though delivered with a usual calm demeanour, had struck a chord, reinforcing the nagging doubts that had been simmering beneath the surface of Eleanor's optimism.

She decided to delve deeper into Seraphina's background.
Eleanor contacted her old university friend, Penelope, a meticulous researcher but, more than that, a friend from what she now considered her old life. She let out a laugh at the thought when just a few weeks back, she was living a semi-normal existence, and here she was, something straight out of a horror movie. She deeply needed contact with her old life for grounding, if nothing else.
After several hours of feverish online research, Penelope unearthed a few tantalising tidbits: Seraphina's father, a renowned physicist, had disappeared without a trace several years prior, his research into temporal mechanics abruptly ceasing.

The more Eleanor learned, the more confused she became.
Was Seraphina genuinely attempting to atone for her father's sins? Or was this meticulously planned act of contrition a cleverly disguised infiltration tactic, a way for the Synarchy to gain access to their opponents' strategies and undermine their efforts? The possibility that Seraphina might be a double agent, playing both sides against the middle, felt increasingly plausible.
The next few days were a blur of clandestine meetings, coded messages, and frantic information gathering. Eleanor and Seraphina continued to work together, their partnership a delicate dance between trust and suspicion. They shared

information, compared notes, and meticulously planned their next move: a daring infiltration of a Synarchy compound, a hidden facility nestled deep within the countryside. It was step one.

The Synarchy's time-travel machine, its sinister purpose still shrouded in mystery, posed an existential threat to Eleanor and her loved ones and the entire country.

As the day of the infiltration approached, the tension mounted. Eleanor found herself constantly assessing Seraphina's every action, looking for subtle clues, for the slightest hint of deception. She observed the way Seraphina held her teacup, the slight tremor in her hand; the way she avoided direct eye contact, as if fearful of revealing something hidden within her gaze. These seemingly insignificant details, amplified by her mounting anxiety, became evidence of deceit in her mind.

During one of their clandestine meetings, a safehouse she had access to from a life of privilege, opposite a graveyard, under the watchful gaze of crumbling tombstones, Seraphina spoke.

"They're watching," Seraphina murmured, her voice barely above a whisper, her gaze fixed on a point somewhere beyond the rain-streaked window. "They have sensed us…. something's shifted. They're tightening their grip."

Eleanor felt a chill, not entirely from the chill wind whistling through the gaps in the old window frame. The sheer power of the Synarchy and their operation's chilling efficiency was a tangible presence in the room, heavy and oppressive.

Trusting Seraphina, a daughter of one of their highest-ranking members, felt like a gamble with fate, a leap into the unknown. Yet, the alternative – continuing to fight alone, adrift in a sea of manipulated minds and warped realities – was simply incomprehensible.

"What can you tell me about the time machine?" Eleanor asked, her voice betraying a hint of the fear that tugged at her. Agnes's map had revealed the locations of several nexus points, but the central mechanism, the heart of the Synarchy's scheme, remained shrouded in mystery.

Seraphina took a slow, deliberate sip of her tea, her eyes distant, lost in the memories that seemed to cling to her. "It's not a machine in the traditional sense," she began, her voice low and hesitant. "It's... an amplification device. A conduit. It draws upon... energies, from multiple sources, to allow an explorer to go back in time."

"Energies?" Eleanor pressed, leaning forward, her curiosity piqued. "What kind of energies?"

She hesitated, choosing her words carefully. "Ancient ley lines, amplified by technology far beyond anything you could imagine. My father always called it 'the resonance.' For them, it's not about having a simple machine to travel through time and observe history. It's about harnessing the flow of time, bending it to their will."

The implications were staggering. The Synarchy wasn't simply manipulating individuals; they were seeking to manipulate time itself.

The widespread despair and the inexplicable suicides weren't random occurrences. They were calculated steps in a larger, terrifying plan.

"And what is their ultimate plan?" Eleanor asked her voice tight with urgency. The urgency was compounded by the frantic barking of Winston from the hallway.

Seraphina's eyes flickered. "To create a new world. A world free from what they perceive as 'weakness,' a world cleansed of... dissent."

"A cleansed world?" Eleanor felt a cold dread creep into her heart. "How?"

"By rewriting history," Seraphina said grimly. "By erasing the past and creating a future entirely under their control. Each suicide, each act of despair, feeds the resonance and strengthens the conduit. It's a horrific, twisted form of societal sacrifice."

The image of the map, the network of lines connecting key locations across Britain, flooded back into Eleanor's mind. It wasn't just a map of influence; it was a blueprint, a roadmap for a dystopian future.

Suddenly, a sharp crack of thunder jolted them, the lights flickered, and Winston's barking escalated to a frenzied howl. Seraphina reacted instantly, grabbing a heavy iron poker from beside the hearth.

"They're here," she whispered, her eyes blazing with a mixture of fear and fierce determination. The seemingly idyllic place was replaced with an eeriness.

"We need to go, stay with me, stay close," she said.

Eleanor fumbled with Winston's lead. A sudden rolling thunder outside diverts the intruders' attention, allowing them a precious moment to escape through the back door.

A series of loud bangs, followed by shattering glass, echoed from the front of the house, and they ran through the forest, running for their lives.

They ran, their breath ragged, the pounding of their hearts echoing the relentless drumming of rain against the leaves. As they fled through the dark, Eleanor caught a fleeting glimpse of a figure standing in the shadows of the garden, a figure who seemed strangely familiar yet impossibly out of place in this desperate struggle. The figure seemed to be looking around with a chilling calmness, their face obscured by the darkness, their presence adding yet another layer of mystery and intrigue to the already tangled web of secrets.

Their escape was narrow, a brush with death that left them shaken but alive. They found temporary refuge in an old barn belonging to Seraphina's family, the air thick with the smell of damp earth and decaying wood. As they huddled together, listening to the sounds of the pursuit fading into the distance, Seraphina said, "My father's colleagues now know that I have betrayed them. We made it out before they could spot you, so you're safe for now. But you need to be careful of who you speak to and what you do. They have eyes everywhere."
The thought crossed Eleanor's mind: was that encounter all a set-up? A show to prove her loyalty to their cause?
Eleanor confronted Seraphina directly. "Why should I trust you?" she asked, her voice barely a whisper. The wind howled through the ancient trees, its mournful sound mirroring the turmoil in Eleanor's heart.

Seraphina's response was unexpected. She didn't offer a carefully crafted excuse or a rehearsed alibi. Instead, she spoke of her guilt, her remorse for her father's actions, and her desperate desire to undo the harm he had caused. She confessed to feeling trapped, manipulated, and forced to participate in the Synarchy's wicked schemes. She spoke of fear, of betrayal, of a life spent walking a tightrope between loyalty and rebellion.

"I know it's hard to believe," Seraphina admitted, her voice trembling slightly. "But I want to stop them as much as you do."

"We need to get to the old cottage, there's some of his things that we need to analyse," Seraphina said.

"The records of the time machine," Eleanor said, her voice firm despite the tremor in her hands. "Where are they?"

Seraphina met her gaze, a spark of hope flickering in her eyes. "Hidden. In a place only a few people know. A place my father believed was safe." She paused, and a small smile played upon her lips. "A place with a rather interesting history, if I may say so."

Unraveling the Family Secrets

They set off on a short journey to a small, forgotten village nestled deep within an obscure place long forgotten. The battered Land Rover, its suspension groaning in protest at the uneven track, bumped its way through the tall trees and rolling hills. Inside, Eleanor clutched the steering wheel, her knuckles white against the black plastic. Beside her, Seraphina stared out the window, her expression a mask of grim determination. The drive from the old barn felt like a hair's breadth away from disaster.

"So," Eleanor began, her voice hesitant, breaking the tense silence, "your father… designed the time travel machine?"
Seraphina nodded, her gaze fixed on the passing landscape. A faint tremor ran through her voice, betraying the years of suppressed emotion. "He believed in their cause. At least, that's what he always told me. Something about restoring balance, correcting the natural order, all that pompous nonsense." A wry smile touched her lips, a flicker of dark humour in the oppressive atmosphere. "He always did have a flair for the dramatic."
Eleanor leaned forward, intrigued. "Balance? Correcting the natural order? That sounds… vague."

Seraphina sighed, running a hand through her already dishevelled hair. "It's a smokescreen, Eleanor. A beautiful, seductive lie that masked something far more sinister. The

Synarchy isn't interested in balance; they're obsessed with control. Control of time, control of people, control of everything." She paused, her eyes darkening. "My father was one of their key architects. He helped design the machine."

The word hung in the air, heavy with implications. The time-travel machine – the weapon that was wreaking havoc on their world, twisting lives and destinies into grotesque parodies of their former selves. Eleanor felt a chill run down her spine. This wasn't just about stopping a shadowy organisation but preventing a cataclysmic alteration of reality itself.

Seraphina hesitated, a shadow passing over her face. "It's a complicated machine, a work of…. It feeds on despair on negative emotions. Each act of self-harm, each suicide, each moment of utter hopelessness fuels its power. It's a grotesque paradox – the more misery it creates, the stronger it becomes." She shuddered as if reliving a terrible memory. "My father always claimed it was a way to 'recalibrate' history, to undo past mistakes, but I know better. It's a weapon of mass destruction, capable of rewriting the fabric of time."

"But… your family," Eleanor ventured, her voice laced with apprehension, "you said they're involved?"

Seraphina nodded grimly. "The Synarchy isn't just a clandestine group; it's a network, a web woven through generations of influential families. My mother's family, the Ashworths, have been deeply entrenched in it for centuries. Their influence stretches far beyond the quaint town we know into the halls of power." She leaned closer, her voice dropping to a conspiratorial whisper. "Think about it, Eleanor. The seemingly unrelated events, the coincidences… they were all orchestrated. The Synarchy subtly works, manipulating events and influencing individuals to subtly steer them towards their inevitable downfall. They're masters of psychological warfare."

"My father," Seraphina continued, her voice barely above a whisper, "he kept meticulous records. Hidden diaries, coded messages… He was planning to leave the Synarchy to expose their treachery. But they found out." Her eyes filled with unshed tears. "They killed him."

The confession hung heavy in the air, a chilling testament to the Synarchy's ruthlessness. Eleanor felt a pang of sympathy for Seraphina, for the burden she carried, for the loss she had endured. But there was also a surge of grim determination. She couldn't let Seraphina's father's sacrifice be in vain.

The Land Rover lurched as it hit a particularly large pothole. Eleanor glanced at Seraphina, her face etched with grief and a fierce resolve. The journey had brought them further than either could have anticipated, but the destination, the final confrontation with the Synarchy, seemed more daunting than ever.

The village was eerily quiet. The only sounds are the rustling of leaves and the distant caw of a crow. The air held a palpable sense of age, a weight of history, that seemed to press down upon them. Seraphina led Eleanor to a seemingly ordinary cottage, its stone walls weathered by centuries of wind and rain.

"My father loved this place," Seraphina said softly as they approached the cottage. "He often came here to escape the pressures of his work. It's the house his grandparents once owned. A place steeped in family history - and family secrets."

The cottage's front door was unlocked. Inside, the air was heavy with the scent of dust and forgotten memories.

Cobwebs draped from the corners of the ceiling and furniture was covered in white sheets. The place seemed to emanate an aura of abandonment. Yet, there was a sense of purpose in its stillness, a feeling that this was not merely a place of decay but of silent, watchful guardianship.

Seraphina led Eleanor through a maze of shadowy rooms, each more cluttered and mysterious than the last. Finally, they reached a small, hidden study. The candle flickered, and she placed it on the dusty desk, casting long, dancing shadows that seemed to writhe and twist, almost as if possessed. And there, nestled amongst ancient books and forgotten artefacts, was a small, iron-bound chest.

As Seraphina struggled with the lock, a sudden tremor ran through the ground. The candle flickered violently, threatening to extinguish itself. The air grew cold, a chilling wind snaking its way through the cracks in the walls. The quiet village outside was momentarily disturbed by an unsettling, low hum. Eleanor felt a prickling sensation on her skin, a feeling of unease, of being watched. Something was approaching, something sinister, something powerful.

"Hurry," Eleanor whispered, her voice barely audible above the growing hum.

With a final click, the chest sprung open, revealing a collection of diaries, photographs, and coded documents. It wasn't just records but a treasure trove of secrets, the key to potentially unravelling the Synarchy's dark history and sinister plan.

She reached into the chest again and produced a small, intricately carved wooden box. "My father kept this hidden," she explained, handing it to Eleanor. "It contains evidence that could bring the Synarchy down." The box felt strangely cold to the touch, its weight heavy with the weight of secrets.

Inside, Eleanor found a series of coded memory sticks, presumably containing documents, detailing the Synarchy's technology, their plans.

The sheer volume of information was overwhelming, but its existence proved Seraphina was telling the truth. Or at least, part of the truth.

They each took as much as they could carry and left, driving back along the country roads and leaving the village and night behind. They ditched the Land Rover in the brushes outside of town and separately made their way back in the dark to their humble abodes. Being seen together would have drawn too much suspicion. Eleanor would update Agnes in the morning.

Eleanor found herself caught in a web of uncertainty. Could she truly trust Seraphina, even now? The possibility of a double-cross, a devastating betrayal at the eleventh hour, remained a constant threat, a chilling undercurrent to their burgeoning alliance. Yet, the weight of the evidence, the gravity of their shared purpose, compelled her to believe for now.

A Risky Gambit

The following day, Eleanor got a message to Agnes, giving her an update on the situation. The documents validated much of the information Agnes had already gleaned, adding critical details that completed the puzzle.

Eleanor explained to Warrick she'd be away for a few days and that he shouldn't worry. Warrick, sinking deeper into himself and his thoughts, chose to bite his tongue and accept that Eleanor was trying to make sense of things beyond their control. He was barely coping under the weight of current events as it was, and he resolved to busy himself staying active and spending time taking photographs of the beautiful town and developing them in his dark room. He found capturing the best images of the town was at dawn - when all was quiet.

Ralph, Wilson and Ivor were tasked with scoping out two other potential properties belonging to the Synarchy.
Eleanor and Seraphina had arranged to meet at an old barn on the outskirts of town. It was another plot of land owned by Seraphina's family. Huddled around a crackling fire, the air, thick with the scent of woodsmoke, offered a temporary reprieve from the chilling reality of their situation.
"Right then," Eleanor declared, taking a small swig of her black coffee, "Operation Infiltration: Code Name – Badger's Bluff."
Seraphina raised a sceptical eyebrow. "Badger's Bluff? Really? Sounds suspiciously like something from a children's adventure story."

Eleanor chuckled, a dry, brittle sound. "It's got a certain...charm, doesn't it? Besides, we need a code name that doesn't exactly scream 'highly trained espionage agents'."

Their plan, born from a frantic brainstorming session fuelled by adrenaline and coffee, would see them infiltrate another one of the Synarchy's quarters, a supposedly impenetrable fortress nestled deep within a seemingly innocuous estate called Blackwood Manor. Their information, gleaned from the diaries and coded documents, hinted at a weakness: during the hours of 13:00 – 14:00 daily, a seemingly insignificant staff entrance was poorly monitored. It was a risky gambit, a long shot with the odds stacked firmly against them. But it was their only shot. "The security footage is minimal," Seraphina explained, tracing a finger across a crudely drawn map of Blackwood Manor, "and the staff entrance is virtually blind. We'll need disguises, naturally. Something inconspicuous. Perhaps...gardeners?"

The next few hours were a whirlwind of frantic activity. They acquired the necessary tools – a rusty pair of secateurs, a battered spade, and a rather suspicious-looking pair of shears – from a disgruntled farmer who seemed more interested in gossiping about the local council than their nefarious plans. Seraphina, surprisingly resourceful, managed to procure a pair of rather fetching overalls from a nearby charity shop.
Their disguises, while hardly convincing, were certainly...committed. Eleanor, with her perpetually windswept hair and a determined grimace, looked like she'd been gardening for decades; Seraphina, with her impeccable posture and slightly too-bright smile, seemed to have fallen out of a rather high-end gardening magazine.

The journey to Blackwood Manor was fraught with tension; it was two hundred miles away, and they couldn't miss the incredibly tight window. They travelled under the cloak of darkness, the Land Rover's headlights cutting through the thick fog like a pair of watchful eyes. Every rustle of leaves, every hoot of an owl, sent jolts of adrenaline through their veins.

As dawn approached, painting the sky in shades of lavender and rose, they arrived at the nearest town and sought to blend in. Stopping at a petrol station, they refuelled their car and then drove round to the drive-through for coffee and some light breakfast. It would be a few hours' wait, and they needed a caffeine fix to get through. They parked up at the local church, where the only sound was of the birds.

As the morning turned into late morning, they browsed the high street and picked up a few supplies, including some unusual-looking flowers they asked to have boxed. "That's a bit of a touch," said Eleanor, nodding to the flowers Seraphina was holding.

At exactly 12:58, they arrived at Blackwood Manor. The imposing edifice loomed ahead, a gothic monstrosity of grey stone and dark windows shrouded in an eerie silence. It was a place that seemed to breathe menace, a tangible expression of the Synarchy's chilling presence.

With their hearts hammering against their ribs, they made their way to the staff entrance gates, which were clearly marked in bold lettering.

As they stopped the vehicle, Eleanor felt her mind drift to another time, another life. The sensation was sudden – a disorienting flash. She was back in another world, a different reality, standing in the rain with Warrick by her side. She could feel the weight of his presence next to her; the warmth of his hand as it reached for hers. They had been running, their hearts in sync, the world collapsing around them.

She blinked, the flash of memory slipping away as quickly as it had come. What on earth was that flashback that I just had, she thought. Was it a memory of a lifelong past?

"Ready?" Seraphina whispered, her breath misting in the cold morning air.

Eleanor, steeling herself again, nodded, her gaze fixed on the gates. They approached with the measured gait of seasoned professionals. Their carefully constructed personas slipped into place–the slightly bewildered gardener and the excessively enthusiastic assistant. The gatekeeper, a surly-looking man with a face like a crumpled newspaper, eyed them suspiciously. He appeared to be more concerned with his crossword puzzle than the two suspiciously well-dressed gardeners attempting to enter the grounds.

"Got a delivery for the groundskeeper," Eleanor said, her voice surprisingly steady, "urgent consignment of... rare hybrid dahlias."

The gatekeeper grunted, barely looking up from his puzzle. "Just get in and get out," he mumbled, barely registering their presence.

And with that, they were in. The vast grounds of Blackwood Manor stretched before them, a labyrinth of manicured lawns, ancient trees, and strategically placed security cameras. The staff entrance, a discreet side door tucked away behind a sprawling hedge, was less impressive than they'd pictured. In fact, it looked more like an afterthought than a carefully planned entry point.

They moved with a calculated stealth, their every step carefully measured, their senses heightened. The air, once thick with tension, now felt heavy with anticipation.
The true challenge was yet to come. Getting in was one thing; navigating the labyrinthine corridors of the manor and reaching their target was another entirely.
The inside of the manor was even more intimidating than the exterior gave the perception of.

Grand, echoing hallways, portraits of stern-faced members, and an overall atmosphere of unsettling stillness created a sense of foreboding. Eleanor and Seraphina moved through the dimly lit corridors, their steps muffled by thick carpets. The silence was broken only by the occasional creak of a floorboard or the distant ticking of a grandfather clock.
They navigated past several groups of staff, each seemingly lost in their own world, oblivious to the two rather out-of-place gardeners lurking in their midst. Their disguises held surprisingly well. No one seemed to question their presence, which was somewhat unsettling and kept Eleanor on guard.
Using their meticulously studied map and a healthy dose of improvisation, they eventually located the location of the Synarchy's time-travel machine – a large, imposing vault hidden deep within the manor's basement. The heavy steel door, secured with a complex lock, seemed impenetrable.
However, Seraphina had a key.

The vault opened to reveal a room filled with humming machinery, flashing lights, and an air of intense energy. The time-travel machine itself was a marvel of both ingenuity and unsettling design – a chaotic tangle of wires, crystals, and gleaming metal pulsing with a malign energy that prickled the skin.

Eleanor felt a surge of fear, a cold dread that threatened to overwhelm her. But she pushed it aside, focusing on the task at hand. Their goal was not to stop the machine, not yet.

Their immediate objective was to gather evidence, to find proof that could be used against The Synarchy. The machine, however, was not their only objective. The diaries suggested another crucial piece of the puzzle, a hidden laboratory deep within the complex, where the Synarchy was experimenting with their sinister technology.

The next 45 minutes were a race against time as they systematically documented their findings, photographing schematics, collecting samples, and searching for any clues that could unravel the Synarchy's sinister plan. They were a long way from being able to stop the machine, but each piece of information they gathered brought them closer to understanding how it worked and could be disabled.

The atmosphere within the vault thrummed with an unsettling energy. Every whirring component, every flashing light, added to the sense of unease. They worked in feverish haste, acutely aware that their time was running out. The weight of the world – or at least, the fate of their quaint corner of the countryside – rested heavily on their shoulders. The risk, the sheer audacity of their gamble, had pushed them to the brink, yet the thrill of the challenge, the possibility of victory, kept them going. The night was far from over, and the true test of their risky gambit was yet to come. The escape, they knew, would be even more perilous than the infiltration.

Unexpected Betrayal

The escape from the Synarchy's subterranean lair was a near-death experience. They navigated a winding network of tunnels, the air growing steadily thinner, the oppressive silence punctuated only by the frantic thudding of their hearts. Seraphina, surprisingly agile, led the way, her knowledge of the facility's layout proving invaluable.

Eleanor stumbled behind, her breath catching in her throat, her mind racing with a million anxieties. The thought of failure, of the machine continuing its horrifying work, was a relentless, chilling presence. Finally, they burst into the crisp air, gasping for breath, their senses overwhelmed by the sudden change in environment.

"We made it," Eleanor whispered, her voice hoarse.

"For now," Seraphina replied, her eyes still reflecting the shadows of their harrowing escape. "But the real challenge begins now."

Their next move was to head to the coast, where the next lair was to be infiltrated. Seraphina had reached out to an old friend of her father's; she lived near the spot they needed to infiltrate, and it was a safe house. It was a risky move for Eleanor, trusting someone new. The Synarchy's reach was extensive; remaining undetected would be extremely difficult. They set off, moving with the stealth and caution honed over the past few days, their hearts pounding with every rustle of leaves, every distant car engine.

Pru greeted them with a nervous smile and a pot of steaming chamomile tea. Pru, according to Seraphina, was a former colleague of her father, a high-ranking Synarchy member, who, due to a severe ethical crisis after a horrific Synarchy-related accident, had made his way to a local monastery in Wales.

This was before he suddenly disappeared. Pru, deeply remorseful about her role within the Synarchy, was now dedicated to thwarting their plans.

As they recounted their experiences to Pru, Eleanor noticed a subtle shift in Seraphina's demeanour. Her usual composure seemed to falter, replaced by an anxious restlessness. She fidgeted with a loose thread on her sleeve, avoiding Eleanor's gaze. The relaxed confidence that had previously characterized their partnership seemed to have evaporated. The details of their escape were recounted, the tense atmosphere hanging heavy between them.

Eleanor nipped to the loo, and on her high-tech burner phone, which scrambled signals, she sent a message to Warrick to let him know she was safe and loved him. He replied he loved her and missed her, as did Winston and that his interview went well. Reading his reply, her eyes welled up, and she stifled them just in time before an all-out bellowing, which felt long overdue. She flopped into bed with the days events replaying in her mind. The Manor entry and sight of the time machine had been a success and she reminded herself the small wins were huge leaps.

The following morning, Pru supplied them with new clothes and new disguises, consisting of wigs and glasses to hide their identity, ensuring the Synarchy's networks wouldn't recognise them. They made their way to the town and planned their next steps. This was when the betrayal manifested itself.

They were in a small café, fuelled by strong coffee and the lingering adrenaline of their close call, discussing their next course of action - acquiring more advanced technology to disable the time machine - when Seraphina received a cryptic text message. Her reaction was immediate and alarming: a flash of fear crossed her face, quickly masked by a practised calm, as she read the message. Without a word, she abruptly excused herself, leaving Eleanor alone.
Eleanor watched, her unease growing with each passing second. Seraphina's sudden departure was far from normal. Something felt deeply amiss.

An hour passed, and Seraphina didn't return. Panic gnawed at Eleanor's insides. She tried calling Seraphina, but her phone went straight to voicemail. A cold dread washed over her. She had placed her complete trust in Seraphina, and now it seemed as though that trust had been catastrophically misplaced.

As Eleanor contemplated her next move, a sense of betrayal cut through her, deeper than any physical wound. The weight of it felt almost unbearable. She had risked her life, trusting a woman whose loyalty seemed questionable from the outset. The seemingly noble cause, the shared purpose, had been a deceptive facade, a carefully crafted ploy for infiltration or even a deliberate act of sabotage.
Suddenly, the coffee shop door opened. A male figure entered. It wasn't Seraphina. Instead, it was a man, tall and imposing, his features obscured by a heavy trench coat and a wide-brimmed hat. He sat at a table near Eleanor, his eyes never leaving her. He spoke in a low, gravelly voice, his words barely audible above the café's gentle hum.

"She's gone to them, hasn't she?" the man said, his voice devoid of warmth, full of a heavy sense of foreboding.

"Seraphina. She's a viper, masquerading as an ally."

Eleanor felt a knot tighten in her stomach. This stranger, who looked like something straight out of a wartime spy thriller, somehow knew what she'd been thinking. He produced a small, battered notebook, a familiar crest emblazoned upon its cover. A symbol associated with a splinter group who had broken away from the Synarchy but couldn't stop them.
"My name is Marcus," the man stated, his gaze unwavering.
"And I believe we have a shared enemy. The Synarchy is far more intricate and insidious than you might imagine."

Marcus explained that Seraphina wasn't simply a misguided ally; she was a double agent, meticulously positioned within the Synarchy's hierarchy, providing them with vital information while feigning loyalty to the rebellious faction. Her betrayal was not an impulsive act but a meticulously planned operation devised over an extended period of decades. There was little doubt she intended to not only derail Eleanor's efforts but also to provide the Synarchy with insight into the strategies and capabilities of the opposition.
He presented her with evidence – photographs of meetings with various members, intercepted communications clearly showing an alliance, and damning details about Seraphina's background. It turned out Seraphina's father wasn't just a high-ranking member. He was one of the key architects of the time machine. His daughter, allegedly his secret weapon, was tasked with maintaining its effectiveness. Seraphina's supposed

remorse was a masterful fabrication, her act of rebellion a deceptive ruse to gain trust and access to critical information.

Eleanor was shattered. The woman she had trusted implicitly, the one who had shared her darkest fears and bravest moments, had betrayed her utterly. The betrayal stung, not just for the loss of an ally, but for the chilling realisation of how deeply ingrained the Synarchy's manipulation was, extending even to those who seemed to offer genuine resistance.
Marcus's appearance wasn't just serendipitous; he had been tracking Seraphina's movements, anticipating her defection. He now offered Eleanor a choice: join forces with him or continue alone, burdened with the knowledge of Seraphina's deception and facing the Synarchy's wrath without any support.

The weight of the decision pressed down on her. Trust, she learned, was a precarious thing, a commodity easily abused and exploited in the treacherous world she had stumbled into. The game had shifted, the stakes had risen, and the lines between friend and foe had become frighteningly blurred. The unexpected betrayal was a brutal lesson, a stark reminder that there were no guaranteed allies in the fight against a powerful and insidious enemy, only shifting Alliances and the constant threat of treachery. The question now was: could she trust Marcus, a man who emerged from the shadows to offer a seemingly unlikely lifeline? And more importantly, would she be able to overcome this devastating blow and continue the fight? The answer remained elusive, hanging heavy in the air, as thick and ominous as the approaching storm clouds.

The Lair

The air hung thick and heavy with the scent of damp earth and something else... something acidic. Eleanor, her heart hammering against her ribs, followed Seraphina through a narrow passage carved deep within the chalk cliffs.

She'd declined Marcus' offer of allegiance but left it open to say she would run it past her associates. He said he would find her again, leaving her feeling very uneasy.

Seraphina returned, but Eleanor never mentioned the encounter with Marcus. Seraphina told Eleanor she'd run off to tend to her mother. Eleanor had to believe her, she had nothing else to go on.

Seraphina said, "We need to go now. I've got us into the cave."

The cave opening was an obscure trapdoor behind a boulder on the coast. What felt like hundreds of steps led down a tight passage. The passage was barely wide enough for two, the rough-hewn walls slick with moisture. Seraphina was surprisingly calm for someone who had suddenly anxiously disappeared only hours earlier.

"This is... rather less salubrious than I anticipated," she muttered, trying to keep her voice low. Even her own breath sounded loud in the confined space.

Seraphina chuckled, a low, throaty sound that was oddly comforting in the claustrophobic setting. "Trust me, Eleanor. The Synarchy doesn't do tasteful rustic chic."

They navigated a series of twisting tunnels, the air growing colder and the metallic scent stronger with each step.

Eleanor saw vast underground caverns, a subterranean city humming with sinister energy. She pictured ancient rituals, arcane symbols carved into the walls, and the chilling hum of technology – a jarring juxtaposition of the old and the new, of mysticism and science. The thought sent a shiver down her spine, even as a flicker of excitement sparked within her. This was the heart of the operation, the lair of the beast, and she was about to face it.

The tunnels opened into various caverns until they finally reached one, illuminated by a sickly green glow emanating from complex machinery. It was a scene ripped from a science fiction nightmare – a chaotic jumble of wires, pipes, and pulsating orbs of light. In the centre, dominating the space, was a colossal machine, a magnificent and terrifying testament to human ingenuity. It resembled a colossal clockwork device but far more intricate and powerful, radiating an unsettling energy that seemed to hum in Eleanor's bones.

"The Chronos Engine," Seraphina whispered, her voice awed yet apprehensive. "They call it that."

Eleanor stared, mesmerised. The machine was the width of a minibus and as tall.

Glowing filaments weaved through its structure like veins, pulsing with an unnatural light, its intricacy both beautiful and horrifying. She could feel the power emanating from it, a palpable force that seemed to warp the basis of their reality. The metallic scent was strongest here, sharp and overwhelming.

They moved cautiously through the cavern, the sound of their footsteps echoing eerily in the vast space. They navigated a complex series of laser grids and pressure plates, Seraphina moving with an almost supernatural awareness while Eleanor, relying on a combination of instinct and sheer luck, managed to keep up.

Around the edge of the cavern, in a dimly lit alcove, they found what appeared to be a control room. Monitors displayed a confusing array of data streams, graphs, and schematics. A large, central console pulsed with the same sickly green light as the machine itself. This was the command centre, the nerve centre of the operation.

"This is it," Seraphina said, her voice strained. "The main control panel."

As Seraphina began to examine the console, Eleanor noticed something peculiar. A small, almost invisible inscription was etched into the side of the console. It was a symbol, ancient yet strangely familiar. It was similar to a symbol she had seen in her grandmother's old collection of antique books – a symbol associated with a forgotten Celtic goddess of sorrow.

The symbolism was deeply disturbing, highlighting the sinister blend of ancient magic and cutting-edge technology that powered The Synarchy's operation.

Suddenly, a harsh, metallic clang echoed through the cavern. The lights flickered, and a chorus of alarms began to blare. They were discovered.

"We need to get to the core of the machine," Seraphina hissed, her eyes darting around the cavern. "There's a way to disable it from the inside, but it's risky."

The lack of manned security was a testament to their arrogance at being so well-connected and powerful, taking out any opposition. They didn't need more than a few tech spiders as security.

Seraphina worked frantically at the console, her fingers flying across the controls, while Eleanor stood guard, her senses on high alert. The atmosphere was charged with tension, the future of the world hanging in the balance. It was a battle against time, a race against the ticking clock of impending doom.

Then, just as Seraphina was about to disable the machine, she suddenly said, "If only you had your mother's knowledge, this would be a cinch."

And as she spoke, the words echoed through the cavern – her mother. Eleanor stared blankly at her, "What do you mean by my mother?"

The Heart of the Machine

The air crackled with a palpable energy, a hum that vibrated in Eleanor's bones. Before them, bathed in the eerie glow of phosphorescent fungi clinging to the cavern walls, stood the heart of the machine – a chaotic tangle of wires, gleaming metal, and pulsating crystals. It resembled a giant, metallic spider, its legs splayed across a raised platform, each ending in a sharp, needle-like point. Writings, etched in a language Eleanor didn't recognise, snaked across the polished surfaces, glowing faintly.

Seraphina, her face pale but resolute, stepped forward, her hand hovering over a small, intricately carved box she carried. "This is the control unit," she whispered, her voice barely audible above the machine's low thrum. "It regulates the temporal flux." She opened the box, revealing a series of delicate levers and dials, each marked with cryptic symbols.
Eleanor, still reeling from the revelation of her mother's involvement, felt a knot of dread tighten in her stomach.
This wasn't just some futuristic gadget. It looked decades old...
The air thrummed with a power that was both terrifying and strangely alluring - time itself was being manipulated within this cavern.
"How old is this thing, and how does it work?" Eleanor asked, her voice trembling slightly.

Seraphina took a deep breath, her eyes fixed on the machine.
"The Synarchy has harnessed... well, let's just say they've harnessed energies far older than our understanding of physics. These crystals," she gestured towards the pulsating

gems embedded in the machine's framework, "they act as conduits. They draw upon... echoes of past events, amplifying them, manipulating them."

"Echoes?" Eleanor echoed, confused.

"Think of it like this," Seraphina explained, choosing her words carefully. "Every event in time leaves an imprint, a faint resonance. The Synarchy has found a way to tap into these resonances, to amplify them, to...rewrite history." She paused, her voice dropping to a near-whisper. "They're not just travelling through time; they're changing it."

Eleanor felt a chill crawl down her spine. The implications were staggering. If the Synarchy could rewrite history, what were the consequences? What had they already changed?

The thought sent a wave of nausea washing over her.

"And my mother is involved in this?" Eleanor asked, her voice tight with fear.

Seraphina nodded grimly. "Your mother is a high-ranking member. She's been a key player in the design of a new system. The Synarchy members all have vested interests in seeing this play out as intended. I am so sorry, Eleanor."

The enormity of it all crashed down on Eleanor. The seemingly random suicides she'd witnessed weren't random at all. They were carefully orchestrated, a macabre ritual feeding the monstrous machine. And her mother... her own mother was complicit in this horrifying scheme.

"What on earth?" Eleanor asked, her voice barely a breath. "Why would she be involved in all of this?"

Seraphina shrugged a gesture that spoke volumes about the complexities of the Synarchy's motives. "Power, of course. Control. The ability to reshape the world according to a warped vision. The members all believe they are creating a utopia, purging the world of its flaws. A world free from... well, from anything that doesn't fit their warped ideology."

Eleanor imagined the faces of those who had taken their own lives, their final moments clouded by despair she now understood was not their own but a carefully crafted illusion, a poisonous seed planted by the Synarchy. The betrayal, the manipulation, was staggering. It extended into the very essence of her life, poisoning her relationships and perception of reality. Seraphina began to explain the intricate process of disabling the machine – a process involving a precise sequence of lever manipulations and carefully inserting a specially designed counter-crystal – a low growl echoed through the cavern. A tremor ran through the ground, causing dust to rain from the cavern ceiling.

"They know," Seraphina whispered, her eyes darting towards the entrance to the passage. "We have to go now!"

Eleanor, her adrenaline surging, helped Seraphina with the delicate task of disabling the machine. The intricate mechanisms seemed to fight back, the pulsating crystals flaring with an angry light as Seraphina worked pushing the buttons, all of which looked foreign and then, with the final button pressed, the air crackled and sparked, and the metallic hum intensified into a deafening roar. The ground shook violently, the very stones of the cavern groaning under the strain.

Suddenly, a blinding flash of light erupted from the machine's core, accompanied by a deafening cracking sound. The entire cavern seemed to vibrate with the force of the energy released. Eleanor felt a searing pain in her ears as the roar intensified, and a wave of nausea washed over her as the reality of the situation slammed into her. This wasn't just a machine; this was a gateway. A gateway to the past, to the future, to a reality fractured and warped by the Synarchy's manipulations.

For a moment, she saw glimpses of shattered timelines, fragmented images flashing through her mind: a distorted version of her own childhood, her mother a cold, calculating figure; alternate versions of herself, living lives she never knew she could have lived; and a horrifying vision of a future where the Synarchy's reign of terror had consumed the country.

Then, as quickly as it had begun, the energy subsided. The machine fell silent, its lights dimming to a faint flicker. A thick silence descended upon the cavern, broken only by the heavy sound of their own breathing. The air seemed thick with the lingering scent of burned plastic and something else... something ancient, something profoundly unsettling.

Seraphina checked the machine, her face a mask of grim satisfaction. "It's done," she whispered, her voice hoarse. "Another one down." She made a gesture towards the exit. "We need to leave."

They ran, the deafening alarms echoing in their ears.

As they sped out of the cavern, through the winding tunnels and back the way they entered, the weight of their discovery hung heavy between them. The Synarchy's sinister plot was thwarted, but the damage they inflicted on time remained unknown. Eleanor knew this was a drop in the unending ocean of their plot. The taste of betrayal was bitter on her tongue. The future, once a predictable path, now felt like a perilous, shifting landscape full of unseen dangers and unpredictable twists. The thought of confronting her mother, an architect of this devastation, filled her with a mixture of dread and a fierce, unwavering determination. The race to prevent the Synarchy's disaster was at full speed.

Unmasking a Leader

The familiar stone house loomed before Eleanor, its windows taking on a darkened sheen, like vacant eyes staring out at the stormy night.

Inside, she knew, resided one of The Synarchy's enigmatic leaders. She clutched the worn journal, its pages filled with cryptic symbols and chilling revelations, a tangible link to the conspiracy that had shattered her world.

She'd spent the last few days piecing together the fragments of information gleaned from the whistleblowers, from the cryptic messages hidden within the Synarchy's own documents, and from her own increasingly sharp intuition. The puzzle had slowly resolved itself, revealing a picture far more sinister and far more personal than she anticipated.

Her footsteps echoed in the silent hallway as she made her way towards the grand oak door at the end. The air hung heavy with the scent of old mahogany and stale cigars. She paused, taking a deep breath to calm her racing heart. This wasn't just a battle against a shadowy organisation; it was a battle against a betrayal that cut to the very core of her being.

The door creaked open, revealing a dimly lit room. A fire crackled merrily in the hearth, casting dancing shadows across the walls. Seated in a high-backed chair, silhouetted against the flames, was a leader of The Synarchy. But it wasn't the austere, faceless figure she'd expected. It was her mother.

Eleanor's breath hitched in her throat. The woman, her face etched with a weariness that belied her age, looked up, her eyes – the same shade of startling blue as Eleanor's own – holding a mixture of sorrow and steely determination.

"Eleanor," her mother said, her voice a low, melodic hum that somehow managed to both soothe and unsettle. "I knew you would come."

"Why?" Eleanor whispered, her voice trembling slightly.

Her mother sighed, a sound like wind rustling through autumn leaves. "It began with a desire for something...more," she confessed, her gaze distant. "A world free from the limitations of time, free from the constraints of fate. The Synarchy's idea, at its inception, was a noble pursuit. We sought to understand the flow of time to harness its power for the good of humanity. But...after some time, I learned to appreciate the true power lay in the future, not the past. We needed to find a way to see the future and alter it to our advantage to prevent another empire from becoming the power. Power corrupts, as they say. I want you to know my intentions were good."

She gestured towards a complex array of instruments carefully on display around the room, a room which held so much familiarity but until then held little resonance. Gleaming crystals, intricately carved metal devices, and objects she'd seen and never placed any importance on until now.

"The machine," her mother explained, "was intended to heal, to mend the fractured timelines. To prevent tragedies, to right wrongs. But we lost control. We underestimated the consequences."

"Lost control?" Eleanor echoed, her voice laced with disbelief. "You destroyed lives! You unleashed despair and suicide! To fuel your sick, twisted ideal of a world you thought you should own."

Her mother flinched, a flicker of pain crossing her face. "Not intentionally," she whispered. "We believed we were saving more people, that we were creating a better future. We were blinded by ambition, by a thirst for knowledge that proved too intoxicating."

Eleanor felt a surge of anger, a white-hot rage that threatened to consume her. "And the lies? The manipulation? My friends, your own family...they were all pawns in your game!"

Her mother's eyes filled with tears. "They were collateral damage," she said softly. "Necessary sacrifices to achieve our goal."

"What goal?" Eleanor pressed her voice tight with fury. "What ultimate purpose justifies all this suffering?"

Her mother leaned forward, her voice dropping to a conspiratorial murmur. "Imagine a world without war, without poverty, without disease. A world where every mistake, every tragedy, could be undone. The human race could evolve beyond its limitations and inherent flaws."

Eleanor stared at her mother, trying to reconcile the idealistic vision she once held with the horrific reality of the woman standing in front of her. It was a seductive argument, a utopia, but there was no reconciling. It would be built upon a foundation of deceit, unimaginable cruelty and mass loss of life.

"But the flaws in everyone's lives were created by The Synarchy, so that doesn't add up!" Eleanor said, her voice filled with a chilling calm. "You unleashed hell at the cost of free will, of individual choice, at the cost of countless lives. How does that benefit humanity in any way?"

Her mother looked away, her gaze falling on the flickering flames in the hearth. The silence that followed stretched, heavy and suffocating, broken only by the crackle of the fire.

The weight of her betrayal, the sheer magnitude of her actions, seemed to crush her.

Eleanor stepped closer, her eyes fixed on her mother's face. "It ends tonight," she declared, her voice firm, resolute. "The Synarchy is over." she attempted to reason with whatever humanity remained.

"You need to put an end to this. Surely, you see that your actions are evil."

Her mother looked up, a flicker of defiance in her eyes. "I've protected you from them, but you have overstepped, and they're going to find out you're against them. You need to leave now before they come. I do love you, Eleanor, but I can't give up on this dream. Get out of here, now."

The centuries of secrets and betrayals raced through Eleanor. Her grandmother had tried to warn people but was ignored and subsequently murdered. Her own mother hid that from her entire family. Her mother, her own mother, was the gatekeeper and complicit in the murder of an unknown number of people. Eleanor, driven by a mix of grief, rage, and an unwavering commitment to justice, vowed to stop them. "I will never let you get away with this," she said, and she ran, ran as fast as she could until she couldn't run any further and let out a scream, one which emanated from her stomach and through her heart - it was her battle cry.

Revelations

She contacted Seraphina and arranged to meet her at the old barn. She lit the fire and watched its embers begin to glow. She turned to see a shadowy figure in the doorway. It was a woman, her face etched with the weariness of centuries, her eyes holding a depth of sorrow that chilled Eleanor to the bone. Her silver hair cascaded down her shoulders like a shimmering waterfall, framing a face both beautiful and frightening in its intensity. Eleanor recognised the elegant lines of the silver locket she wore – a locket identical to the one her grandmother had bequeathed her, a locket that had been mysteriously missing for years.

"Eleanor," the woman said, her voice a low, melodious hum, "I hoped we would see each other again."

The revelation hit Eleanor like a physical blow. This woman, this figure standing in front of her, was her grandmother, or at least, a very convincing double. The resemblance was uncanny, but the air of malevolence emanating from the woman made it impossible to deny a crucial difference. The grandmother Eleanor heard about was a kind, if slightly eccentric, woman who loved gardening and birdwatching. This woman exuded a power that felt both ancient and primal. Her grandmother's diary spoke of being afraid of the Synarchy. Her grandmother had been deceased for years.

"How... how is this possible?" Eleanor stammered, clutching the journal tighter.

The woman smiled, a slow, chilling curve of her lips. "Oh, sweet darling, Eleanor," she purred, "some things are more complicated than they appear. Family secrets, you see, have a way of lingering, of weaving themselves into our lives at the most opportune moments."

The woman proceeded to unravel a tale that spanned generations. It was a story of ambition, betrayal, and a thirst for power that defied the boundaries of reason. Esther explained that The Synarchy was not simply a shadowy organisation but a lineage, a bloodline stretching back centuries, each generation adding to the insidious machinery of control. They had perfected the art of manipulating time, not through advanced technology alone but through a blend of ancient rituals and technological innovation. The crystals, it turned out, were not just artefacts but a nexus, a point where the energies of time converged and stored. They held purpose.

Esther explained how the time-travel machine, far from being a simple device, was almost a living entity fuelled by negative emotions – despair, hopelessness, and suicide. Each act of self-destruction fed the machine, strengthening its power and extending its reach into the past and the future. The manipulation of the villagers, the subtle psychological warfare, and the seemingly random acts of strange behaviour were all part of a grand design, a twisted experiment to harvest the energies of despair.

And then came the heart-stopping revelation: they weren't simply manipulating Eleanor's town. She was testing it, observing its resilience. The entire country had unknowingly been a testing ground for the perfected system of manipulating time and emotion, a real-world laboratory for their nefarious plan. This was a controlled experiment, and Eleanor, unwittingly, was its subject.

Eleanor's shock morphed into a cold, hard fury. The betrayal stung, not just from the deception itself but from the shattering of her perception of her family history. Her grandmother, the woman she'd respected, was not the kindly birdwatcher but the architect of this unimaginable horror.

"You used my family, my friends," Eleanor hissed, her voice shaking with a mixture of rage and disbelief. "You used them as pawns in your sick game."

Esther shook her head, a gesture that revealed a coldness that ran deeper than any physical chill. "Sentimentality is a luxury not all can afford, Eleanor. Sometimes the end justifies the means, and the Synarchy's end is the ability to control time itself."

Eleanor's mind raced, trying to process this onslaught of information. Esther, the younger version, was her grandmother from an earlier time, and Esther, standing before her much older, was also her grandmother, as she would have been. They'd morphed time? Or they could switch between times at will? The Synarchy's manipulation wasn't just about power; it was about a distorted desire to control time. They were playing God, and Eleanor was caught in the middle of their cruel game. But unlike the public, she knew the rules of the game. She had seen the hidden mechanisms grasped the intricate web of deception.

But there was another layer to this intricate plot. Esther revealed a hidden truth, a secret even she hadn't fully understood until recently. The locket, the identical locket that Eleanor once possessed, wasn't merely a family heirloom; it was a key, a vital component within the larger time manipulation apparatus. Its unique properties, a subtle resonance with the crystals, held the potential to disrupt the Synarchy's control.

The locket, Esther revealed with a chilling smile, contained a tiny sliver of a meteorite, a fragment that held immense power. It resonated with the crystals' energy in a way that amplified both its destructive and potentially restorative capabilities. She'd held the power to either destroy the system or weaponise it.

The unexpected presence of the locket, a cherished family keepsake, added a personal stake to Eleanor's fight. She had to confront her family legacy and choose between inheritance and destruction. The weight of this decision pressed down upon her, heavier than any physical burden. The game had shifted from one of infiltration and discovery to a high-stakes battle for control of time itself.

The conversation continued late into the night. She'd taken the name of Seraphina, her friend inside the cabal, a young woman she'd grown close to, a confidant.

In her chillingly calm manner, Esther laid bare the history of The Synarchy, revealing intricate details of their plans and the chilling extent of their influence. It extended far beyond the quaint countryside, influencing national events and shaping political landscapes, all operating from the shadows.

Eleanor learned of their elaborate network of spies, informants, and collaborators, each playing a part in the grand scheme of time manipulation. She learned how the Synarchy manipulated information, subtly altering historical accounts and influencing political decisions to secure their power.

With a hint of weary sadness, Esther explained that the Synarchy wasn't driven entirely by malice but by a warped belief in the ability to control their and everyone's destiny. They saw themselves as the guardians of time, its rightful rulers, entitled to reshape it as they saw fit. Their actions, however monstrous, were justified in their own corrupted worldview. This added a layer of complexity to Eleanor's mission; it was no longer a simple case of stopping a villain but of confronting a warped ideology that had spanned centuries.

The revelation of her grandmother's identity, or the identity of the woman who claimed her grandmother's lineage, shattered Eleanor's perception of her family history. Once cherished memories now held a bitter taste of betrayal and manipulation. The woman she'd been led to believe was one of harmony and identifying birdsong was, in reality, a cold and calculating mastermind manipulating events on a wide scale.

As the first rays of dawn painted the sky a pale grey, Eleanor felt a profound sense of exhaustion mingled with a steely determination. She had faced her worst nightmare, confronted her family's dark secret, and discovered a power she never knew she possessed. The locket, once a symbol of familial connection, now represented her only hope against the Synarchy's sinister plan, the key to potentially unlocking the power to restore time to undo the damage done.

She had a choice to make, a terrifying choice that would determine not just her fate but the fate of the world. The fight, she knew, was far from over. The first plot twist revealed a devastating truth, but the journey towards justice was far from complete. The path ahead was fraught with peril, corruption, deceit and hidden agendas, but Eleanor, armed with the truth, was ready to face it.

The Time Loop

"I need to show you something," Esther said. "Here, step this way."

They left the old barn and through the gate at the edge of the trees, Esther opened a trapdoor.

"Don't be frightened, trust me."

Feeling deeply uneasy but curious to learn the truth of everything, Eleanor followed her grandmother.

The air in the Synarchy's hidden bunker hung thick with the sickly sweet scent of despair. Eleanor, her breath catching in her throat, stared at the swirling vortex of chaotic energy at the heart of what appeared to be a large round hologram, a more high-tech version of a very large lava lamp. Another time-travel machine? It pulsed with an ominous, hypnotic rhythm, a thrumming heartbeat in the subterranean silence. Esther, her face pale but resolute, stood beside her, her hand resting on the hilt of a surprisingly elegant, antique dagger tucked into her belt. It seemed wildly out of place amidst the futuristic technology surrounding them.

"This is a travel portal. You can travel anywhere that another portal exists; currently, there are about 200 in the country that I'm aware of. These are how they travel between places so quickly."

"So people could turn up here?"

"They could, but it isn't on the portal map, so they'd need to know about it, and no one does, apart from us."

Eleanor, strangely curious but acutely aware she would be using a contraption owned by the enemy.

"Here, hold my hand. I'm going to show you something." As much as she felt repelled by taking her own grandmother's hand - given her revelations - she also had an insatiable need to know the truth.

She stood beside her grandmother in another of the cabal's lairs. This room they were in held what looked like a similar time machine they'd destroyed in the cavern. Of course, they had multiple machines. How could Eleanor have been so naive? Agnes had been right about her assumptions.

"This machine is capable of creating Time loops," Esther whispered, her voice barely audible above the machine's low hum. "It doesn't only send some people back in time; it's capable of trapping them. It can be programmed to repeat the same timeframe, whether 10 days or more, over and over, until…" she trailed off, her eyes wide with a horror that went beyond the simple fear of death. "Until they break."

Eleanor shivered, a cold dread gripping her. The implications were terrifying. Targeted people, anyone deemed undesirable by the order, would be sent into a perpetual time loop of despair. It wasn't only the manipulation of history but the systematic torture of countless individuals trapped in an endless cycle of their own personal hells. The chosen victims weren't simply erased; they were broken, and their spirits ground down until they were nothing but hollow shells. The Synarchy wasn't just changing history; they were slowly, methodically dismantling the very anatomy of human resilience.

"How does it work?" Eleanor asked, her voice strained. She felt a familiar surge of adrenaline, the cold, sharp edge of fear sharpening her senses. This wasn't just about stopping a conspiracy but about rescuing countless souls from a living nightmare. Esther explained the mechanics of the loop, her words a stark contrast to the chaotic energy of the machine. It appeared the machine didn't simply transport individuals through time but rather anchored them to a specific point, a temporal anchor that would reset.

The victims were subjected to the same experiences and the same choices, leading inevitably to the same outcome: a slow descent into madness, culminating in despair so profound it further fuelled the super time machine's horrific power.

"They're not aware it's a loop at first," Esther continued her voice tight with emotion. "The initial shock, the trauma, it's so overwhelming, they don't even register the repetition. But after a few cycles… the repetition becomes a crushing weight. They know. And the knowledge alone is enough to drive them to the brink."

The horror of it settled on Eleanor like a physical blow. She could almost feel the crushing weight of those endless repetitions, the despair clinging to her like a shroud. The faces of her husband, friends and neighbours flashed before her eyes, the possibility they could end up in an even worse situation than they were in, getting pushed into this time machine.

The thought sent a chill down her spine. They needed to stop the machine, not just for the sake of history but for the sake of all those trapped within its vicious grasp. But how?

"What do we do? How do we break this machine?"

The machine was complex, a terrifying tangle of ancient lines and sinister-edge technology with its whirring sound and energies causing a disquietening feeling deep within her. It appeared almost living, a grotesque parody of life itself.

"With these, I've collated these. They're the antidote we need for this machine. It's the ancient salt of a long-lost Middle Eastern plain combined with the positive memories of all who have entered, which were stored within the machine and I extracted. Those two combined, captured within this vessel, will send the machine into a state of confusion and cause an overdrive. Your grandfather was a good man, Eleanor. He helped create the machine, but he found his conscience and set out detailed notes in his diary, the antidote to this machine."

"You've lied about who you are. Your entire story is a lie. Why are you helping us to stop this if you benefited from it all the years? Why return to the here and now?" Eleanor cried.

"When I returned a few weeks ago, it was to put an end to all of this. I saw you, all grown up and caught a glimpse of myself in you. You and I are so alike, and I realised we had a small chance of achieving what I could not do alone. And that's when I approached you. You read my diary. I was a young mother with a daughter whose husband had recently passed. Everything had gone: all of our money, our stability, our future. When I discovered there was something amiss going on, I'd been experiencing some awful level of shit, as was everyone around, but everyone else seemed oblivious. My husband's lineage was part of the Synarchy. He was instrumental in designing the machine but was misled to believe the negative energy was something different. When he learned of their ultimate plans for the machine, he was horrified, and he knew too much, so they murdered him. I knew none of that.

My research began in a similar vein to yours, presumably. We notice things and spot patterns. I wrote my diary as evidence in case anything happened to me. Then I had an idea: the only way for me to get to the truth was to join them. So I began contacting everyone I thought could get me an in, starting with my husband's family. I had to feign interest, which was the hardest thing for me to do.

What I hadn't realised at the time was the scale of the operation, and as I gained the trust of the higher-ups, I was told about the time travel machine. I was horrified; truly, I was. At first, anyway. Then, it dawned on me that I could go back in time and prevent my husband's murder without fully understanding the implications of that. I had to be patient as the machine wasn't ready. Yes, I later learned what fuelled the machine and accepted my part. When the time machine was ready, we had a trial run. I was one of the first explorers. The requirement, was to test the machine, to observe history in its entirety and report back. There would be no alterations made. That was the rule set by your grandfather in his original blueprints. The machine's capability was such that it could send someone back in time, but they could only return to the present time the world had moved onto. There was no future functionality to it. We couldn't move forward in time - to a time yet to be lived. But that is what they're testing right now. The new prototype is in the final stages."

She let out a heavy sigh and then continued. "I went back," her eyes darted across the room. "and I saw your grandfather – and could only observe. It was gut-wrenching. I had to relive the loss, watch it all unfold again...and it broke me."

Eleanor could feel the sadness emanating from her grandmother's words. "It was an enormous responsibility raising your mother whilst reconciling what I was doing in what should have been our time together, playing the role that I'd become...On my final journey, I went back too far and discovered that we are not here on this earth alone. I found the existence of God, Eleanor, whatever God may be, a Higher being. I felt God in my soul speak to me, and it was here that I learned I'd corrupted my own soul. I returned to the present time, only to find my life had been altered, somehow in the mix, I'd warped time. I was able to switch between the here and now and the past, but at a huge cost, as you know. So I made a choice. Your mother, oh God, loves her, Eleanor, don't hate her. In the intervening years was recruited by the Synarchy due to her lineage, and I wasn't there to prevent it. So you see, she's only partially to blame for her part...and you and I truly are on the same side." she smiled.

The hum of the machine intensified, a rising crescendo of violent energy that vibrated through the floor and into Eleanor's very bones, Esther's shocking revelations sending Eleanor's mind into overdrive.

Esther pointed to a panel shimmering with an array of flashing lights. "That's the temporal displacement regulator," she explained, her voice tight with urgency. "If we can overload it, we might be able to scramble the temporal field before it can rewrite anything." She was helping her to stop the machine.

Eleanor felt like a spectator in her own life, watching as two women, attempted to avert a catastrophe of cosmic proportions her own family were instrumental in causing - in a damp, subterranean bunker. The absurdity of the situation, the madness of it all, she was in shock.

"We need to bypass the primary power conduit," Esther said, her brow furrowed in concentration. "It's shielded, heavily protected, but there's a secondary access point..." She tapped a sequence of codes into a hidden keypad, the metallic click echoing eerily in the confined space. "It's a bit of a gamble. If we miscalculate, we risk everything."

Time seemed to stretch, minutes feeling like hours. The air grew thick with tension, a palpable energy that crackled between them like static electricity. The hum of the machine reached a fever pitch, the swirling vortex at its heart growing brighter, more intense until it seemed to threaten to consume them both.

Esther let out a sharp cry of triumph. "I've got it!" she yelled over the roar of the machine. "The regulator's bypassed. Now, we need to overload it..."

With a practised ease that surprised Eleanor, Esther sent the vessel through the opening, the action causing a blinding flash and a deafening roar. The machine bucked and vibrated, the temporal vortex flickering erratically before collapsing in on itself, imploding with a deafening crack that reverberated through the bunker.

"Esther! What the hell are you doing!" roared a voice echoing with the power of a thousand tormented souls. "You think you have the right to interfere with the natural order?" He whipped out a dagger.

Esther, protective of her granddaughter, challenged the man to a fierce battle.

"This is anything but natural, and I have every right. You killed my husband, and you've stolen countless lives."

Esther shouted as she lunged at him with surprising ferocity, her small antique dagger suddenly extending into a medieval sword, flashing in the dim light, her movements fluid and precise.

Eleanor, fuelled by adrenaline and a fierce determination to save her grandmother, found an unexpected strength within her. She grappled with the Synarchy's leader, a brutal, desperate fight that tested her physical and mental limits.

Just as the Synarchy's leader gained the upper hand on Esther, There was a deafening roar, a blinding flash of light, and then… silence. The machine sputtered, its chaotic energy collapsing in on itself. The vortex of swirling energy disappeared.

Silence. A heavy, profound silence, punctuated only by the ragged gasps of their breathing.

Then, a low, groaning sound emerged from the heart of the machine, a sound of strained metal and collapsing energy. The machine was dying.

Exhausted but strangely exhilarated, Eleanor and Esther leaned against the console, their bodies trembling. They had done it. They had stopped the machine.

The air itself felt lighter, cleansed. The feeling of oppressive despair that had permeated the room lifted. But the victory was bittersweet.

A head of the Synarchy had been defeated. He was knocked out and bruised but alive.

Esther and Eleanor stared at each other In a vague embrace, In a time that was real to Eleanor. A growing respect, even a hint of affection, began to replace her shock. Perhaps Esther was indeed a genuine ally, a woman struggling against the darkness, striving to make amends for the sins of her father.

But the freeing of countless souls from their temporal prison had come at a price for Esther. She disappeared before Eleanor's eyes, caught in a time travel paradox of her own making. She was gone, lost to someplace in time. Eleanor didn't know whether she would see her again. Esther and the locket holding the piece of meteorite had gone missing.

Eleanor, shaking with adrenaline, a head of the Synarchy knocked out but fully aware of his presence, ran again and drove all night and this time she didn't stop until she reached the safety of the safehouse.

Reaching the safe house, a sprawling but unassuming cottage nestled amidst rolling hills, hidden amongst trees, was a relief that bordered on euphoria. Inside, she lit the fire, which began to crackle merrily, casting dancing shadows on the walls, creating a comforting contrast to the horrors she'd faced.

She sent Warrick a concise message - he was no longer safe where he was, to trust her and provided the cottage location. Bring supplies, but don't delay and leave straight away.

She spent the next couple of days with her husband and dog, sleeping, recovering, and being in her loved ones' presence. The shock of her family being involved, the unnatural life and world around her she'd been living through, which had become her reality, was a head fuck of epic proportions, and she needed time out. She caught wind that her mother was missing. The thought crossed her mind: she'd used a time machine to avoid the repercussions of her decisions.

As she exhaled, she realised the safehouse now belonged to her and Warrick and that she'd ensure it was used as a source for good when it was all over.

She told Agnes and the team that we'd bought ourselves some time. But it's only a temporary reprieve. We need to find a way to dismantle the entire operation, expose them before they can rebuild, and find their other machines and destroy them. Then, we need to expose them for the monsters they are.

Agnes replied, sent her condolences about the revelations and clarified she'd had no idea about Eleanor's family involvement. She was as shocked, but she vowed they would continue the fight. Stopping the Time Loop machine had been a monumental task, a terrifying race against time, but it was merely the next step in a much longer, far more complicated fight. The Synarchy had underestimated her, underestimated them all. They had underestimated the resilience of the human spirit, the strength that could be found even in the face of unimaginable horror.

As they sat by the fire, the weight of their ordeal began to settle upon them. The adrenaline began to fade, leaving behind a profound exhaustion that settled into their bones. Eleanor looked at her husband. There was a silent understanding between them, an unbreakable bond.

When Eleanor was ready, she began to tell him the entire story. He listened to her carefully whilst Winston lay between them. It was a tale not of fiction but of a very real, disturbing reality that wasn't going to vanish, and life as they knew it before was no more. Things would never be the same for as long as the Synarchy and all its accomplices were in power.

"This feels like something out of a bad film," Warrick said.

Eleanor tried to force a smile, but that quickly faded. "Yeah, a really bad one."

"Well, we can't let fear decide our fate. We'll come up with a plan," The fear receded as determination took its place.

"With a little help from our Winston," he said, touching Eleanor's side.

"What if I told you I'd been having flashbacks and… they aren't just dreams? What if I believe they are memories? Memories from a past life? Memories of us fighting this same fight against the same enemy?"

Warrick raised an eyebrow, "Past life? Seriously?" He let out a low whistle. "Okay, let's take it back a step."

"No, listen," Eleanor pleaded, "I've found more evidence.

Ancient texts, cryptic symbols. The patterns match. Everything that's been taking place - it's all connected. It points to something ancient, something powerful, something that spans centuries." She pulled out a book, a book she'd found in her research, its pages filled with faded script and strange symbols. "This book, I think, holds some of the knowledge that souls do indeed exist and that we really do hold inherent, ancient knowledge within us, and the way to access it has been deliberately hidden."

Warrick, intrigued despite himself, hesitantly took the book. He flipped through the aged pages, his sceptical expression slowly giving way to something akin to fascination. The strange symbols, the intricate drawings, the ancient language– it was unsettling yet captivating. It whispered of a hidden history, a forgotten war, a conspiracy that stretched far beyond their suburban cul-de-sac.

He studied one particular drawing: a swirling vortex of dark energy, a strangely familiar symbol, a feeling of déjà vu washing over him. The same symbol was etched into a silver locket he'd seen his wife wear, one she'd always claimed was just a sentimental heirloom from her grandmother.

"This..." he murmured, tracing the intricate lines with his finger, "This looks like..." He hesitated, searching for the right words. "Like something from... one of my dreams."

A small, hesitant smile played on Eleanor's lips. A crack in Warrick's wall of cynicism had appeared, a tiny fissure in his stubborn disbelief. It was a beginning. And Warrick, tempered by the mounting evidence and a shared memory of a dream, possibly even a past life, was finally, just barely, beginning to see the truth. The time machine was real. The past lives were real. The Synarchy was real. The conspiracy was real.

But as she held his gaze, the ache deepened. Another flash came - sharper this time. It was a vision of the two of them in another lifetime, another place and explosions were going off in the distance. They were running, side by side, in a world much like this one but far more brutal. The same determination in their eyes, the same sense of purpose in their movements.

Warrick was beside her, his arm extended toward her and pulled her under a bush to save her life.

The vision was gone in an instant, but the fear lingered.

She turned to Warrick, a soft smile tugging at her lips. "We'll make it through," she said, the words for both of them, even if she wasn't sure she could believe them.

She pulled a small journal from her side. "My grandfather's notes," she explained, her voice hushed. "They contain details about The Synarchy's origins, their methods, and their ultimate goals. Coupled with all our research, all the information we have collated, might be our only way to bring them down permanently. To prove, via their own heavily controlled media systems, unequivocally how far back they go, how deeply entrenched in worldly operations they are and how sinister their plans are. The entire blueprints to their operation are almost wholly known."

Eleanor leaned forward, her heart pounding in her chest. She knew that the data they held was the key to their victory, but she was also acutely aware of the danger of holding that data. The knowledge in my grandfather's journal pages could very well cause a much larger conflict.

The fire crackled, casting flickering shadows on their faces as they began to delve into the mysteries contained within the journal's aged pages. The race against time was far from over. The real battle had just begun. The fight to expose The Synarchy, to dismantle their nefarious network, to ensure that the horrific future they had glimpsed would never come to pass, was now fully underway.

Unsettling news

The flickering firelight jumped across Warrick's determined face as he traced a finger across a faded diagram in the ancient journal.

"That," Eleanor announced, her voice hushed but resolute, "is the key. It details the Synarchy's network of informants and collaborators – the people who unwittingly, or perhaps willingly, help them maintain their grip on power." The diagram was a bewildering tangle of lines and symbols, connecting seemingly disparate individuals and locations across the countryside.

Eleanor leaned closer, her heart pounding a frantic rhythm against her ribs. She recognised a few names – Mrs Higgins, the seemingly innocuous baker with her perpetually sweet smile. Mr Peters, the Vicar and Mr Abernathy, the retired Colonel. The revelation was unsettling, a stark reminder that appearances could be deceiving. The idyllic small-town life she had always cherished was now shrouded in a chilling layer of deception.

"We need to approach these individuals cautiously," Eleanor warned, her eyes scanning the intricate web of connections. "Some may be manipulated, others may be complicit.

Identifying the difference will be crucial." She pointed to a particular symbol, a stylised serpent coiled around a staff. "This signifies those under the direct influence of the Synarchy's technology. They are the most dangerous, their minds clouded, their actions unpredictable."

"We will find a way through this and turn this nightmare into our story of triumph. Together," Warrick said, confidence flooding his voice.

"Together," Eleanor echoed, her heart swelling with hope. They turned to one another, ready to tackle the challenge that lay ahead, knowing that no matter what, they would face it side by side.

Their first contact was a surprisingly unlikely ally; Barnaby Field, a dark haired, blue eyed, middle aged eccentric, known for his unwavering belief in conspiracy theories and his collection of unusual artefacts. Always in shorts and a t shirt no matter the weather, and known to carry around an empty decanter, having quit drinking some years prior. While dismissed by most as harmlessly delusional, Eleanor believed Barnaby possessed unique insights into the Synarchy's activities. He'd been muttering about "temporal anomalies" and "men in black suits" for years, a chaotic stream of pronouncements that suddenly took on a frightening new relevance.

She told Warrick to stay put, and she put on a disguise. She dressed as a plumber, with an old wig found in the closet and overalls she'd used on their garden mission. Finding Barnaby was easy enough; he frequented the pub, The Crooked Spoon, perpetually nursing a pint of water and engaging in increasingly heated debates with the barmaid about the merits of using anti-spyware against government surveillance.

He was, as always, surrounded by a cloud of cigarette smoke and a palpable air of seemingly endless anecdotes about freedom, tyranny and increasingly sinister government intrusion. Why hadn't Eleanor thought to contact Barnaby earlier?

Approaching Barnaby, given the current uncertain atmosphere, would require subtlety. Fully aware he'd have been a prime target for the Synarchy and his awareness of conspiracies, Eleanor approached him at The Spoon Pub and asked if he would accompany her to the private back room, as she had some things he might be interested in.

It began as a polite chat about local folklore and historical oddities. Barnaby, initially suspicious, warmed up to the polite inquiry, his eyes glittering with an unsettling mix of cunning and fear.

"Have you ever wondered if the stories we read are just thin veils over the truth? Is our literature hiding secrets about our world? She began.

Barnaby turned with an intrigued smile, "Ah, Eleanor! Every book is a portal, you know. Who's to say that Charles Dickens wasn't actually writing a coded message about the Illuminati?" Eleanor half smiled.
" True, what if A Christmas Carol was actually a warning about time travellers..." She let the words hang in the air.
Barnaby, nodding seriously, "And Scrooge was literally re-writing his own history. It's what I've been saying all this time: things aren't what they appear to be, and we're given snippets of the truth to downplay the bigger truths."
Eleanor nodded slowly, "It does make one wonder, are we living in a web of hidden agendas and secret societies?" she exhaled.
"I believe we have one right on our doorstep. I've seen things," Barnaby said.

Eleanor's approach seemed to be the right level for Barnaby, as he revealed a surprising wealth of knowledge, recounting overheard conversations, whispered rumours, and fragments of information that, when pieced together, provided vital clues about the Synarchy's operations.

He spoke of clandestine meetings in the old mill, held under the cover of darkness, of hushed voices and strange symbols etched into the walls. He even described a device similar to the one they had encountered at the old manor house, humming with an unnatural energy. He claimed it emitted a low, persistent thrumming that seeped into people's dreams, twisting their thoughts and pushing them to act against their own will. His ramblings, once dismissed as mere eccentricity, now carried the weight of terrifying truth. He'd been protecting himself by staying grounded, relying on his intuition, eating healthily and keeping everyone entertained down the pub. "Can't break someone who is aware and isn't afraid of anything," he delivered with a cheeky smile.

Their next ally, even more surprising, was the spinster known for her prize-winning Seville marmalade, Maeve, and her even more prize-winning collection of secrets. Eleanor was welcomed into the house, and Maeve seemed surprisingly sharp again.

"I pulled myself out of this horrible fog, Eleanor. It's not my age. Something is going on." she said.

"Oh, Maeve, I know. I am so pleased you're back." she touched her arm affectionately.

Maeve, initially resistant, became a valuable source of information after Eleanor shared some of their findings.

Eleanor withheld the majority of the Synarchy's operations to protect everyone's interests, including Maeve's.

Intrigued by the mystery surrounding the recent spate of strange occurrences, Maeve, with her unparalleled knowledge of the town's social intricacies, provided her with a detailed account of each person's movements and relationships.

Maeves' insights helped them to identify individuals who might be unwittingly aiding the Synarchy. She detailed the habits of those she knew, their daily routines, their unspoken alliances, revealing a hidden network of connections that had gone unnoticed before. She highlighted those who had exhibited subtle behavioural changes, becoming withdrawn, secretive, or inexplicably distant from their loved ones. Her tight-lipped nature, once a source of amusement, now proved to be a surprisingly powerful weapon in their fight against time.

Their investigation led them to another unexpected ally: Professor Armitage, a retired University don, a renowned expert on ancient Celtic mythology. He had initially dismissed Eleanor's claims as outlandish. Still, after reviewing the cryptic symbols from the journal and the strange occurrences in the village, he agreed that something extraordinary was happening.

Professor Armitage's expertise proved invaluable in deciphering the cryptic symbols, linking them to ancient rituals and practices designed to manipulate time and energy.

He explained the methods, describing how, historically, societies were curious and experimenting with exploiting energy fields to control minds and influence human behaviour. "If this Synarchy has invented this time travel machine, it's unlikely just a futuristic invention; it would be a sophisticated amalgamation of ancient and modern technology, a perverse synergy of arcane knowledge and cutting-edge science."

Eleanor already knew this but what she found interesting was he'd drawn the very same conclusion from looking at the facts. Professor Armitage went further, "The potential consequences of the Synarchy's actions – a rewriting of history, the eradication of entire timelines, the annihilation of the present. The unnatural disorder it would create is unfathomable. If this is true, Eleanor, it is imperative they are stopped to prevent the obliteration of reality itself."

She returned to her safehouse undetected, having developed a unique set of skills, following the stream, using the hidden tracks and backpaths through the forest.
She reiterated what she'd learned. The Synarchy was powerful, its reach far-reaching, its methods insidious.
Eleanor, Warrick and their allies faced a formidable foe that played on human weaknesses, exploited vulnerabilities, and manipulated reality. The race against time had reached a critical juncture where the slightest misstep could prove fatal.

The additions to their team, the combined strength of the eccentric, the woman who held many secrets, the professor and the determined team, felt surprisingly potent, a strange alliance forged in the fires of impending doom. The next phase of their battle would require strategic precision, unwavering courage, a perfect blend of intellect and intuition, and a symphony of unlikely allies determined to confront the looming darkness. The fate of their world, their reality, hung precariously in the balance. The ticking clock was their relentless enemy, and the stakes, as they had grimly discovered, were impossibly high.

Sacrifice and Loss

The weight of the world, or at least the weight of the impending apocalypse, pressed down on Eleanor's shoulders.

The flashbacks had become more frequent and more vivid. They'd discussed seeing glimpses of other lives – sometimes Eleanor was a healer, tending to the sick in a medieval monastery; Warrick, a scholar or a farmer, tending to his crops. Sometimes, they were soldiers, fighting side-by-side in a brutal war.

These fragments of shared memories were more than just coincidences. They felt deeply connected, deeply personal and inexplicably intertwined, revealing a soul-deep connection that transcended their current existence. They spoke of a bond forged across lifetimes, a destiny interwoven across the tapestry of time itself.

The shared past life flashbacks gave their fight a new layer of urgency. It wasn't just about exposing the conspiracy; it was about something far larger that threatened their lives and the mechanisms of their shared existence - a divine will.

Their shared past lives, it seemed, weren't random to their current experience, making them uniquely positioned to understand and counteract the conspirators' plans.

The flickering candlelight cast long shadows across the worn oak table, highlighting the grim determination etched onto their faces.

Wilson, began to reveal more about the occult aspects of the conspiracy. He explained that the conspirators were concealing hidden secrets about the planet, the truth about the pyramids, the origins of humanity and, indeed, time. They had discovered a unique formula through ancient dark forces that sought to be the ultimate rulers of the planet.

Eleanor and Warrick opened up about their past life connections. Agnes, Wilson, Ralph, Trevor, and Ivor had too, been having flashbacks.

Wilson had been researching and had found scripts which supported the idea that this was perhaps not their first meeting, nor their second – but rather a reunion of ancient spirits who have danced the cycles of many lives. They were all scholars, rebels and healers, warriors and always lovers. The group had joined not by chance but by design.

Each time, though the circumstances differed, the essence of their connection remained unchanged - a magnetic pull that defied logic, that defied time itself in a world where time bends, and the threads of fate intertwine, warrior souls drawn together by a force far greater than human comprehension - the work of a higher being. This ancient force has guided their journey through countless lifetimes. They hadn't met by chance. Their stories were meticulously crafted by an intelligence transcending time and space. In every life, moment of pain, and joyous reunion, they have been mere players in a cosmic war, written by unseen hands that have shaped their every step and nudged them toward each other.

From the beginning, the higher being set their souls on this path, intertwining their destinies in a way that no mortal force could ever hope to control. The higher being knew their souls needed to learn the skills to prepare them for the wars against the darkness each lifetime. The battles were endless; they were brutal, but they were not punished; they were prepared. The higher power, unseen yet ever-present, was always helping to guide them. There were signs, and many of the dark forces would be there to thwart their success at every turn.

The higher being's hand was in their every choice - whether they realised it or not.

Memories of their past lives flickered in dreams, fleeting glimpses of faces, of places, of emotions so vivid they could almost touch them. These memories were not random but pieces of a puzzle that, once assembled, would reveal a complete picture of who they were - and who they were meant to become together. Together, they stood on the precipice of something profound, their combined wisdom helping them navigate the challenges with a determination and resolve they never knew they held. A cumulation of countless lifetimes - each one preparing them for this moment, for this life, where they would fulfil a destiny they have been unknowingly walking toward for eons.

Every hardship they faced, every obstacle they overcame, was a lesson in love and sacrifice, leading them closer to their ultimate purpose. The power behind their connection does not demand, nor does it impose its will. It merely whispers gently when they need to hear it most. Their union, a cosmic alignment, a coming together of forces to help shape the framework of humanity, for peace to one day be realised across all nations and people.

Their lives held a larger purpose, something which echoed through the ages. The higher being had chosen them for a reason - chosen them to face the enemy head-on, and armed with this innate intuition and knowledge, there was no turning back.

Wilson's revelations surged through their hearts and they sat in bewildered silence, contemplating the unusual circumstances they found themselves in. A few months ago, they were living an average existence, filled with trials. Still, if someone had told Eleanor in a few months' time, she'd learn she'd been a warrior in a past life and pre-destined to save humanity in this life, she'd have laughed at the terrible tea leaf reading and told them to jog on.

The shared past experiences gave everyone a new understanding of their present struggle. Their conspirators' actions were not only a threat to their current lives but an assault on their collective history. The cabal was not just seeking to manipulate time; they were trying to erase it, to rewrite the narrative of human existence and replace it with one of utter domination and control.

Their understanding of the shared past lives unlocked a new level of collaboration within the team. They acknowledged that their individual skills and experiences, spanning millennia, were crucial in defeating the cabal. Wilson's deep understanding of their past warrior lives slowly being revealed and shedding light on the dark's motives, a powerful and evil force.

"We need to act," Eleanor said to the room, her voice low, a tremor betraying her carefully constructed facade of calm.

They all voiced their agreement.

It's time for everyone here to be made fully aware of the sinister reality of this nefarious group. "The time-travel device... it's not just about altering the past; it's about erasing it for everyone, rewriting our collective history to suit their nefarious purposes for world domination indefinitely, for the future, never to be removed from that position. And the energy source... it's feeding on despair, on the very essence of human suffering."

The chilling implication hung heavy in the air. The Synarchy wasn't just controlling people; they were harvesting their misery, feeding it into a machine that threatened to unravel the very foundations of time itself. The stark reminder of the personal and collective cost of their mission.

"The order is selecting targets, specific targets."

"There's a pattern," Eleanor continued, her voice catching slightly. "The targets... they're not random. They're strategically chosen, individuals who possess the strength, the resilience... the potential to disrupt the Synarchy's plans."She traced a finger along the diagram, her touch lingering on a specific symbol. "This one... this is Mrs Higgins's son, Ashton."

A wave of nausea washed over Eleanor. She continued, "We all know Ashton. He's a good lad. His own mother is part of the conspiracy. He is strong, resilient, and fiercely loyal to his family young man. He possesses a strength of character and an unwavering commitment to his community that, according to the script, makes him a dangerous anomaly to the Synarchy's insidious plans of control.

"Mr. Holsworth explicitly told me they're not what they seem. We haven't had any contact with all these people for a while. We need to act quick. We need to get them to safety," fear etching into Eleanor's voice.

"We need to get to them," Warrick spoke, his voice firm. "But how? The Synarchy is everywhere, their influence pervasive.

His mother is involved and watches his every step, no doubt. We are no doubt watched too."

Eleanor looked at Warrick, a deep well of conflicting emotions swirling within her. The reality of the situation dawned on her with crushing weight. Protecting Ashton meant putting herself, and potentially her entire family, in mortal danger. The sacrifice was a bitter pill to swallow, but inaction was not an option.

Their strategy involved a complex manoeuvre. They needed to reach Ashton before the Synarchy could exploit his inherent resilience, before they could drain him of his very essence, turning him into another broken, empty husk in their network of controlled despair. And Mr. Holsworth, who was undeniably a soft target.

The plan was set, and Eleanor, Warrick, Barnaby and Ralph travelled under cover of darkness, utilising hidden routes only known to a select few, relying on a network of unlikely allies – and Trevor and Ivor's hacking skills to disrupt the surveillance tech in the town temporarily. He wouldn't be able to hold off the firewall penetration indefinitely; the system was far too big, but he could give them a window of 35 minutes.

The closer they got to the Higgins' farm, the more palpable the Synarchy's influence became. A strange, oppressive stillness hung in the air, a chilling silence that amplified the ticking of the clock, a relentless countdown to disaster. The landscape seemed to shift and change under the cloak of night. Twisted branches of ancient trees reached out like skeletal fingers, the air heavy with an unspoken tension, a palpable sense of something deeply wrong.

They found Ashton in his barn, surrounded by his beloved animals, his usually bright eyes clouded with an unsettling, vacant stare. He barely recognised them, his speech slurred, his movements jerky and uncoordinated. The Synarchy's insidious influence had already begun to take its toll.

There was no time to waste. Ralph and Eleanor carefully placed a rag around Ashton's mouth whilst Barnaby and Warrick grabbed his arms. There wasn't much of a fight. He was despondent.

Next, they pulled up at Mr Holsworth's cottage. There was a dim light in the kitchen. His wife came to the door looking chirpy.

"Hello, so sorry, Mrs. Holsworth, but I have a flat tyre," said Warrick. "Can I borrow your good man, and I'll bring him back soon? Might take a while."

"Certainly, he could probably do with some male presence, he's hardly left the house for weeks," she replied, smile plastered on her, eyes devoid of emotion.

"Thank you. I will be in touch in the morning. Don't worry in the meantime. Just know that he is safe."

"What do you mean? Of course, he is safe," she responded.

"I'll give you an update in the morning. All will be well." Warrick reiterated.

She smiled her bright smile. "That's wonderful, thank you."

Whew, he thought, she couldn't have been weirder. He'd finally seen the behaviour, something unusual happening at night involving her husband, and she was peachy about it.

Under cover of night, the men took Ashton and Mr. Holsworth, and they all made their way back through the backroads to their safe house.

Ashton, his eyes devoid of life, was safe from his mother and the Synarchy's clutches. Mr Holsworth was fairly chatty in the car, almost relieved to be heading into the unknown with his neighbours. The following morning, they'd begin undoing the damage, the psychological torment they'd both been going through. They'd been hard at work on the plan. It involved talking, lots and lots of talking, positively to take them out of the despair.

The safe house became their den, their refuge and their lab, creating, designing and implementing. They were a team and a formidable alliance against a formidable enemy. The cottage was spacious, with enough bedrooms and space to plan, and the private grounds stretched into hundreds of unkept acres. Ralph, along with Trevor and Ivor's tech skills, had set traps securing the property's perimeter. They couldn't be certain the cabal had yet discovered the property. The traps were deadly. They weren't playing a game of chequers; it was survival, life or death, and although they hadn't yet killed anyone, they weren't going to take any chances with murderous cabal trespassers.

Dust

The chilling truth that Seraphina was, in fact, Eleanor's grandmother, Esther, hung heavy in the air, thicker than the fog rolling in from the North Sea. Her own mother being involved was a sickening blow and more than Eleanor could bear. She stared at the intricate diagrams scattered across the table, the candlelight reflecting off the sweat beading on her forehead. The journal, its secrets spilt forth, revealed the Synarchy's horrifying plan – not just to manipulate time, but to rewrite it, erasing swathes of history to suit their nefarious purposes. And Seraphina, her supposed ally, was a key component in this devastating scheme. Her lineage and her selfless assistance… all carefully constructed. But she'd shown herself at the eleventh hour, following a crisis of conscience or the dawning realisation that travelling through time, living in different times and as different people, wasn't as she'd imagined it would be – living meant watching her back, whichever reality she chose. And she'd found evidence of God's existence, forcing her to acknowledge she'd become the very thing she'd sought to eliminate.

The initial shock gave way to a chilling calculation. Esther held a vital piece of the puzzle, a piece that Eleanor had unwittingly overlooked. The woman possessed a deep, almost intuitive understanding of the time machine's mechanics. It wasn't just her knowledge of its underlying principles; it was something more – a visceral connection, feeling as if she was part of its construction. This revelation sparked a flicker of hope amidst the despair. If Esther understood the machine so intimately, then there might be a chink in its seemingly impenetrable armour. A vulnerability that could be exploited.

They needed to understand Esther's connection to the machine to unravel the hidden weakness that could be its undoing. This wasn't merely about stopping the Synarchy; it was about wresting control of time itself from their clutches. Their fates rested on the ability to decipher Esther's cryptic knowledge.

Winston, their beautiful, understanding dog, whined softly, nudging Eleanor's hand with his wet nose as if sensing the weight of the situation. He was a constant, comforting presence amidst the chaos, a testament to the simple joys that the Synarchy sought to obliterate.

Eleanor's mind raced, piecing together fragmented clues. The journal's cryptic entries hinted at a specific component within the machine, a seemingly insignificant part that Esther had subtly emphasised during their discussions. It was a small, almost invisible crystal embedded deep within the machine's core, described in the journal as a "harmonic resonator." Esther had referred to it casually, almost dismissively, yet her tone held a peculiar resonance, a subtle hint of something concealed. Eleanor recalled a fleeting conversation about the crystal's sensitivity to specific frequencies, which were not mentioned anywhere in the available schematics. It was a detail that had initially seemed insignificant, a minor technicality amidst a sea of complex equations. But now, it was a beacon, a lifeline in the suffocating darkness.

The next few hours were a blur of frantic activity. The team worked together to unearth ancient texts and scripts they had and cross-referenced them with every piece of valuable scientific data they held. It was a lot of unravelling. There was a resounding resonance, they'd found the evidence detailing the properties of the crystal. It was far more than a mere resonator; it acted as the main conduit, a focusing lens for the immense energies powering the time machine. The texts revealed a hidden vulnerability: the crystal was susceptible to a specific type of sonic resonance.

This frequency could disrupt its harmonic balance and ultimately destabilise the entire machine. It was a chink in the Synarchy's meticulously crafted armour, a point of failure that they had seemingly overlooked – had her grandfather not spotted this vulnerability or had he simply overlooked it?

The discovery was exhilarating, a surge of adrenaline cutting through the bone-chilling fear. But the knowledge was useless without a practical application. The frequency needed to be precisely calibrated, a task that required specialist equipment and expertise.

They had no choice but to enlist more people. As risky as it was, they needed manpower and they needed expertise outside of their realm of knowledge. There were hurried phone calls, frantic meetings, and the exchange of cryptic messages in dimly lit pubs, the very air thick with the weight of their desperate mission.

Finding the equipment proved relatively straightforward; locating someone with the expertise to calibrate the frequency was a different matter entirely. Finally, they found their specialists through a circuitous route involving Professor Armitage's contact, a retired astrophysicist in The City and his contact, a reclusive musician with an uncanny ear for sound. Jim, the astrophysicist, had access to a laboratory in his basement.

Eleanor would be the one to meet him, Warrick would accompany her, and they'd travel disguised as builders.

The laboratory's chaotic collection of wires, tubes and arcane instruments was a testament to his unconventional genius. But amidst the apparent chaos, there was a method. He listened to Eleanor's frantic explanation, his brow furrowed in concentration, pausing occasionally to hum a tune. This strange, otherworldly melody seemed to resonate with the very walls of his laboratory. Then, he produced a device, a marvel of intricate engineering, a sonic disruptor capable of generating the precise frequency needed to neutralise the crystal's power. The relief was almost tangible, the weight on their shoulders lifting fractionally. The discovery of the machine's hidden weakness had shifted the balance, offering a sliver of hope in a seemingly hopeless situation.

The next challenge was two-fold. They would infiltrate The Synarchy's headquarters, hidden deep within a seemingly innocuous village. Eleanor, armed with her newfound knowledge and aided by Esther's surprisingly detailed insider knowledge (a twisted irony considering the circumstances), Eleanor devised a plan. The team, an unlikely alliance forged in the crucible of impending doom, prepared for their confrontation. The mission was deceptively simple: disarm the machine, destroy it and destroy all prototypes and knowledge to obliterate its existence. The path to success was littered with obstacles – both visible and concealed. The Synarchy was not merely a collection of misguided individuals; they were masters of manipulation and deceit.

They'd meticulously analysed the data, identifying patterns and connections that had previously escaped notice, while Barnaby,

Trevor and Ralph used their charm and charisma to navigate the treacherous social landscape, gaining the trust of unexpected allies. Agnes, Wilson, Dr Albright, Eleanor, and Warrick analysed and pulled together all the historical documents—each working on their own projects toward a common goal.

"What are you working on?" Eleanor asked one evening.

"We're just trying to optimise our misery. Make our suffering a little more efficient," Trevor replied. "If it works, we definitely have a good shot at this."

"It's a highly charged, miniature explosive device, one hopefully capable of causing some irreparable damage." Ralph chipped in.

They were prepared. Their confrontation came not in a fiery clash of weapons but in a subtle manoeuvre, a meticulously organised take-down designed to minimise collateral damage.

It took weeks of meticulous planning, infiltration, and data analysis, and finally, they had it. Irrefutable evidence of the cabal's corporate links, now a much wider issue, meticulously compiled, would be disseminated to the right people, individuals who held enough sway and influence to make a difference.

The journey to the estate was fraught with tension. The countryside, usually serene and picturesque, felt menacing, its beauty a cruel mockery of the impending disaster. Even Winston, lately the epitome of canine calm, seemed to sense the gravity of the situation, his usual playful demeanour replaced with an unusual stillness. The approach to the estate felt like walking towards a precipice, the weight of their mission pressing down on them with unrelenting force. As they neared their destination, a wave of unease washed over them, a palpable sense of impending doom. It wasn't merely the threat of the Synarchy; it was the knowledge that they were playing a deadly game against time itself. The ticking clock, a constant reminder of the stakes involved, fuelled their determination.

The infiltration of the Synarchy compound was set for the following night. Eleanor, alongside the team, had meticulously prepared. They'd studied the blueprints obtained from the wooden box, memorised security protocols, and planned escape routes. The mission felt like a walk across a minefield, every step potentially leading to disaster.
The atmosphere was tense, a thick silence punctuated by the occasional nervous cough or a whispered instruction.
Eleanor stole glances at Warrick, his face etched with a mixture of determination and fear. His eyes, once so enigmatic, now revealed a vulnerability that resonated with Eleanor's own apprehension. This was a fight to preserve their future, a future they had barely begun to build.

The plan was for half the team to stay behind, and at a specific point, they were to release all the data to every independent news outlet, grassroots organisation, contact, and key social media site, flooding the net with the hard evidence of the cabal's plot. This would undoubtedly lead to infighting as the leak would contain high-level documentation.

"The old adage: A house divided against itself cannot stand. We need to make enough of a misdirect to let them trip over their own tangled wires and faulty circuits," Trevor said.

"Use their own divide and control tactics against themselves by pitting them against each other. They'll never discover the origin of the leak as we've got a failsafe in place." Ralph said with a smirk.

"This is going to work," Warrick added, glancing at Eleanor.

They devised a plan to ensure minimal security presence at the Manor by creating a series of diversions. The plan was developed by Ralph and Ivor using deepfake technology. They used the recorded voices from the first meeting they infiltrated and created AI deepfake voice synthesis to impersonate high-level officials. They would call the Manor, informing the security to attend to a matter a few hundred miles away. A carefully timed phone call to the other location would inform them of their required presence. While that was taking place, they'd send a series of overwhelming network traffic, mimicking a DDoS (Distributed Denial of Service) attack, causing their monitoring systems to crash. And as they'd be struggling to regain a hold, they'd send in "security" in the form of Ralph, Ivor and Warrick to take over, simulating a legitimate security sweep, distracting any skeleton crew whilst Eleanor Wilson carried out the task of destroying the time machine. The tech team would pretend to inspect the cameras and sensors, whilst disabling them. Security would believe all systems were functioning as normal whilst reconfiguring surveillance and access points.

As they approached the compound, under the cloak of darkness, Eleanor couldn't shake the feeling of impending doom. The vast, imposing structure loomed before them, a silent testament to the Synarchy's power and malevolence. The air crackled with an almost palpable sense of dread, a foreboding that settled deep in her bones. Were they walking straight into a deadly ambush? The question, unanswered, echoed in her heart, adding a layer of suspense and uncertainty to the already perilous mission.

They hid their vehicle in the forest before disembarking. Eleanor felt she was standing on the edge of a cliff, overlooking a verdant valley, aware of the importance of this confrontation, which would determine the fate of countless people trapped in the Synarchy's insidious plot.
Before her, the Synarchy's headquarters, a technical marvel cloaked in rustic charm – pulsed with an unsettling energy.

Infiltrating the grounds of the estate proved more challenging than anticipated. The base security systems at the gated entrance, while not overtly advanced, were surprisingly effective. Eleanor relied on Esther's passed on knowledge of blind spots and security protocols for Trevor and Ivor to put their plan into action.

Her partners stood around her, her usually composed demeanour laced with a palpable anxiety. The shared experience of near-death escapes and betrayals had forged a bond between them, a fragile alliance built on mutual desperation and a shared thirst for justice.

Eleanor held the sonic disruptor, the one which held energies capable of destroying the feedback loop, the same as the meteorite in Esther's locket. The locket still missing, along with Esther. It was a long shot, a desperate gamble, but it was all they had. The Synarchy's reliance on advanced technology and their arrogance in their own superiority might be their undoing.

"Ready?" Eleanor asked, her voice barely above a whisper yet carrying a steely determination that belied her apprehension. They all signalled, eyes reflecting the flickering lights within the headquarters.

"Here," Trevor passed Warrick what appeared to be a cigarette lighter and a small plastic box. "Ivor and I have been working on a little project. Get this into the machine in case that sonic disruptor fails. Not that I'm suggesting it will...but that in your hand is a failsafe."

"Thank you," Eleanor smiled.

Warrick sighed a huge sigh of relief. "Oh, thank God." he chuckled.

"Alright then, it's do or die time, folks." Ivor delivered with a grim smile.

They split off into two teams. Moving with practised stealth, Eleanor and Wilson, honed by weeks of near-constant peril, navigated the corridors like pros. Eleanor knew the layout, and as they navigated the maze, their tech team were in, systematically cutting off laser grids with the precision of seasoned spies, silencing alarms with a quiet efficiency that spoke of their spectacular technical advancement.

The closer they got to the heart of the operation, the more palpable the tension became, the humming of the machine growing louder, more insistent.

The final chamber was stark, cold and clinical, a stark contrast to the quaint exterior. At its centre sat the time-travel machine, a monstrous contraption of gleaming metal and deafening pulsating lights that seemed to suck the very air from their lungs.

Inside the main chamber, the time machine hummed. It stood as a monument to human ambition gone awry, a testament to the twisted minds of those who sought to control the very fabric of existence. The atmosphere crackled with barely contained power, a tangible sense of danger hanging in the air. Eleanor felt a shiver run down her spine from the cold and raw, untamed energy radiating from the machine. This was no mere invention; it was a force of nature, tamed and harnessed by those who shouldn't possess such power.

She turned to Wilson. "We need to reach the inner core. There's an opening to the side on the diagram here, and the wires connecting must not be damaged before entry," she showed Wilson who nodded in agreement.

"We have 10 minutes."

"Here," he said, "hold this," he passed her the sonic disruptor.

"I'm going to try to disable the gateway from the other side, as this is the route in."

"Be careful," she said.

Confrontation

"Who dares trespass into our sanctuary?" The voice was a hiss laced with icy contempt. "You, insignificant imbeciles, challenge the architects of destiny?"

The Synarchy's leader, a figure Eleanor had recognised from a long-forgotten family photograph, stood before it, his back to them, his silhouette a dark, ominous presence against the machine's eerie glow.

Eleanor, her voice unwavering, replied, "You have played God for too long. Your reign of terror ends tonight."

The leader chuckled, a sound devoid of humour echoing through the chamber. "Your arrogance is admirable, if misguided. But your efforts are futile. The time-travel experiment is far greater than this. It is irreversible. You are ants against a tidal wave."

"The tidal wave is heading straight for your cabal. We've destroyed the only Time Loop machine and all of the data to rebuild it, the accelerator and, as we speak, your latest invention, and all of this is being relayed to the public at this very moment. You've got years of rebuilding, but it won't be easy when you're all behind bars." Eleanor delivered obtusely.

"Not too bad for ants," spat Wilson.

Eleanor turned to see the rest of the team and felt a wave of relief.

The cabal leader turned, revealing a face lined with a chilling mixture of arrogance and despair. It was a face that held a disturbing familiarity, a subtle resemblance to Eleanor herself. Whoever he was in their lineage, she didn't care to find out.

Warrick and Ivor launched themselves at the man. Trevor and Ralph took on one of the security who had been doing a round and had rushed in.

Eleanor, using her intimate knowledge of the machine's workings, disabled several key components, slowing the machine's chaotic energy. This gave the team the crucial opening they needed. With a calculated move, Wilson aimed the sonic disruptor directly at the machine's central core.

The resulting explosion was deafening, a blinding flash of light and a surge of raw energy that shook the room. When the dust settled, the time-travel machine to send people to the future lay in ruins, its sinister hum replaced by a deathly silence. The air, once heavy with dread, felt lighter, cleansed.

The leader, battered but not broken, launched a desperate, final attack. It was then that Warrick leapt onto the leader with a speed and agility that belied his size.

Everyone piled on. The distraction allowed Eleanor to deliver the final strike, sending him unconscious. He was neutralised.

The Machines Destruction

The farmhouse hummed, a darkened heartbeat slowing, then stuttering. Inside, the air thrummed with the dying breath of the time-travel machine – a colossal contraption of gleaming brass, sparking wires, and arcane symbols that looked disturbingly like ancient dialects. The smell of burning filled the air, mingling with the earthy scent of the woods around them.

Warrick's gaze settled on an almost insignificant-looking light. It pulsed with a faint, rhythmic light. As he approached, a holographic projection flickered to life, revealing a figure seated behind an opulent desk, a sinister smile playing on their lips. The image was crystal clear, defying the destruction around them.

"Impressive, wouldn't you agree?" the figure purred, their voice echoing through the chamber. "You managed to disrupt a minor operation, but you've only scratched the surface. I applaud your tenacity, but your efforts are ultimately futile."

The figure revealed themselves to be Dr. Evelyn Reed, a renowned physicist and Nobel laureate, a woman whose name was all over the news, synonymous with groundbreaking scientific advancements and huge governmental influence. She was the government's lead scientific advisor—the person to oversee the health and welfare of the entire country.

They stared, speechless. Evelyn Reed, the darling of the scientific community, the face of innovation and progress, was also the mastermind behind the conspiracy.

"You... you were behind all of this?" Ralph stared at the hologram, disbelief evident in his voice.

Evelyn chuckled, a dry, brittle sound that sent shivers down their spines. "Oh dear," she said, her voice laced with a condescending amusement. "You are all so out of your depth here. It's comical."

"You evil bitch! You've destroyed lives."

Ignoring Ralph's outburst, Evelyn continued. "The world has reached a point of critical mass. Overpopulation, resource depletion, environmental collapse."

"The large organisations, quangos, should be forced to pay to repair the damage they created!" stated Eleanor calmly, belying her fury. "The government should be imposing tighter controls on their pollutive endeavours. But they're not. You're a fraud, nothing more than an evil murderer."

Evelyn, in a chillingly calm tone, replied. "We need to cull the herd. It's a necessary evil—a painful but ultimately effective solution. By harnessing the negative energy generated by the populace, we can achieve the unimaginable, as you've discovered – which is the ability to travel through time. Isn't that magical?" not hiding the cold calculation in her eyes.

Time travel. The grand ambition, the ultimate prize. The reason behind the orchestrated misery. The countless lives ruined, the families torn apart, the deaths of millions of people - all mere stepping stones on the path to achieving the sinister goal.

"What's the purpose of you travelling through time?" Warrick asked, the question hanging in the air, heavy with anguish.

"The future, my dear," Evelyn replied, her smile widening. "A future where we can right the wrongs of the past. A future where humanity is not doomed to destruction. A future where the worthy survive. And those who are deemed worthy are chosen by me."

"So, you're a self-proclaimed god?" Wilson sneered, his voice dripping with sarcasm.
Evelyn only laughed. "Let's just say I have a higher purpose. A responsibility that demands absolute control. It may seem brutal, but it is the only way to ensure the survival of humankind."

They all exchanged a look, a silent conversation passing between them. They were facing not just a criminal mastermind but a woman who believed, with unshakeable conviction, that her actions were for the greater good.

"And how exactly do you plan on achieving this 'greater good'?" Ralph asked, his voice laced with a steely determination. The initial shock had worn off; now, anger was starting to simmer beneath the surface.

"Through selective elimination, of course. Only the strong, the resilient, the spiritually fit will survive," Evelyn explained, her eyes gleaming with a chilling conviction.
"The rest... are undesirable. The machine is a filter to separate the wheat from the chaff. Those who succumb to despair and break under pressure are simply... eliminated by their own weakness."

"You're sick! You're destroying innocent people's lives through mind control. They're not succumbing to despair through weakness. You're manipulating their brainwaves so they're no longer who they are. They've been depleted, deliberately unwittingly, by nefarious people. This has nothing to do with saving humanity. You get sick enjoyment from seeing people suffer to further your twisted desire to time travel." Trevor said, his voice unable to contain his vitriol.

Evelyn waved a dismissive hand. "Collateral damage. A necessary sacrifice for the survival of the species. It's a simple equation, really. And, once I achieve future time travel, I can rewrite history, undo past mistakes, and create a perfect future, a world free from the flaws and failures of this one."

The chilling machiavellian logic of her words sent a wave of nausea through Eleanor. She realised that Evelyn wasn't a typical villain driven by greed or power; she was a lunatic, an evil maniac hiding in plain sight, the country unable to see her true wickedness. Her evil lay in her ability to trick the country into believing she was good when she was the monster humanity needed to eliminate for its future survival. This was more than ultimate power. It was about eugenics on a mass scale. This was an act of mass murder disguised as a noble cause.

She wasn't saving humanity. She was orchestrating its destruction.

Suddenly, a piercing alarm blared, shattering the tense silence. "Intruders," a robotic voice announced. "Security breach."

Evelyn's smile vanished, replaced by a look of cold fury. "It seems our little chat has been interrupted. Unfortunately, this means our conversation must conclude. But don't worry, our paths will inevitably cross again." The holographic image flickered and died; security would be returning in no time, and they needed to get out of there.

Their garnered knowledge of the facility's secret passages and hidden escape routes proved to be the next key to survival. As they made their way towards freedom, Eleanor's earlier anxieties resurfaced, heightened by the immediate and present danger of leaving there alive. The tension was unbearable, a palpable feeling of imminent death weighing heavily on them. Security would be despatched, but they needed to finish what they started.

Eleanor, her heart pounding a frantic rhythm against her ribs, gripped the detonator – a rather elegant, silver device that looked like a cigarette lighter – her knuckles white.
Beside her, Warrick, her husband, a man usually defined by his calm demeanour, nervousness etched on his face. His normally impeccable attire was rumpled, his usually neatly combed hair a mess. The weight of the situation, the gravity of their actions, was etched onto his face.

"Ready?" Eleanor asked her voice barely a whisper, a stark contrast to the deafening hum of the machine, which was now beginning to sputter. She could almost hear the gears grinding to a halt, a mechanical death rattle echoing the internal struggle she felt within herself. The weight of generations, the burden of her family's dark secret, pressed heavily upon her.
Warrick nodded, his gaze flickering towards the ominous device. He squeezed her hand, a silent reassurance passing between them. Their shared history, their years of laughter and quiet companionship, solidified in that moment.

"On my mark," Eleanor said, her voice firm despite the tremor in her hands. The machine's erratic spasms grew more violent, the air thick with the smell of burning metal. Warrick reached out, his hand resting on Eleanor's, and for a moment, a silence felt in their farewell to their normally peaceful life.

"Three..." she began, her voice ringing out with a new found strength, a resilience born out of years of living under the Synarchy's suffocating control.

"Two..." Warrick echoed, his eyes fixed on the pulsating machine. Time seemed to stretch, each second an eternity, as the team held its breath. The humming sound escalated into a high-pitched whine that grated on the nerves.

"One..." Eleanor finished, her voice strong despite the tension vibrating through her body.

Eleanor pressed the button.

A blinding flash of light filled the farmhouse, followed by a deafening roar. The building shuddered, dust rained down and a wave of intense heat washed over them. When the light subsided, a silence descended, a profound silence that was almost more deafening than the preceding chaos. The machine was gone. Not just destroyed but utterly annihilated, reduced to a pile of twisted metal and scorched earth. The farmhouse was, too. The dark energy that had permeated the farmhouse dissipated, leaving behind only the lingering scent of burning. She looked at the team, their faces etched with relief and a comforting, impenetrable bond with one another.

"It's over," Ivor said, breathing a mixture of relief and disbelief in his voice.

They surveyed the damage, a testament to their struggle, a battlefield scarred but ultimately conquered.

The destruction of the future time-travel machine wasn't just a physical act; it was a symbolic dismantling of the Synarchy's power, the breaking of their insidious influence over countless lives. It was a testament to the power of human resilience, a demonstration of the extraordinary strength that can be found in the face of overwhelming odds.

They'd won.

The news spread like wildfire on social media, which both shocked and enthralled the public. There was also massive pushback from the cabal and the news was also denounced to the point that social media was split 50/50.

Eleanor and their team found themselves thrust into defending the truth and keeping it alive on social media. Reluctantly, the news and media outlets were forced to run stories as the media could no longer ignore the news on social media. The news transformed into a national sensation – a blend of thrilling mystery and quirky charm.

A series of raids, arrests, investigations and lawsuits - the alliances with the Synarchy, many exposed and cornered, began to fracture, its once unified power dissolving into chaos and infighting. The team watched in stunned silence as the empire of deceit crumbled behind the scenes. The intricate web that had bound humanity for so long was slowly unravelling.

The reckoning had begun, bringing with it not just the fall of the cabal but the promise of a renewed world built on the foundations of trust and understanding.

The distorted timelines would slowly begin returning to their natural course. The people affected by the Synarchy's machinations would start to regain their autonomy, their memories, and their lives slowly returning to a semblance of normalcy.

The coming days were filled with a whirlwind of activity. Newspapers ran catchy headlines such as "Cottage of The Damned: Unknowns Defeat Time-Travelling Villains" and "A Blast from the Past Saves the Day!"

The inner workings, its methods, and its future plans - if they had any left, were under watchful eyes. The team's testimony and evidence recovered from the destroyed machines, diaries, and everything they'd uncovered allowed law enforcement to unravel the Synarchy's complex network of operatives. But very few arrests were made, despite many investigations launched.

A wave washed over the town as Mrs Higgins, Mr Peters, Mrs Danes, Mr Abernathy, and various neighbours were questioned and arrested on suspicion of subterfuge and treachery, amongst other charges.

There was a long road ahead - repairing the damage, both physical and emotional, left by the Synarchy's influence. The scars of their actions ran deep, leaving a legacy of despair and heartbreak in their wake.

Ashton was slowly making a full recovery, and the town rallied around him, creating a safe space not just for him but for everyone to assist in their collective recovery. Mr Holsworth and his wife were back in a union, and she appeared to be suffering from memory problems.

While the memories of the chaos and the struggle would forever be etched in her memory, she felt a sense of accomplishment, a quiet pride in what she and her allies had achieved. The fight wasn't over. The journey was far from complete. Her own journey of self-discovery and her personal reconciliation with her family's dark legacy still lay ahead. It was a journey she would face, not with fear and not alone.

Many lives had been affected, some irrevocably, by the time manipulation. The Synarchy's tentacles reached everywhere, including large swathes of the market, and their demise caused a domino effect on a number of high-profile finance companies, causing near economic collapse. The markets were failing, which had a knock-on effect for everyone. People were struggling, their finances already in disarray, and despair was setting in - it was an unintended consequence that couldn't have been foreseen in its entirety. The work of rebuilding the trust and the economy would take years. It was another weight on their shoulders.

The media frenzy added another layer of complexity to their situation. They were forced to relive their traumatic experiences through hidden identities, subjected to relentless scrutiny from journalists and pundits eager to dissect every aspect of their story. The constant barrage of questions and the intense pressure to provide simple answers to impossibly complex issues added to their sense of moral uncertainty. They felt like lab rats, dissected and analysed, their humanity reduced to a narrative of good versus evil, a simplistic explanation for a profoundly complicated situation.

In the quiet moments, away from the madness, Warrick and Eleanor struggled to reconcile their actions with their values and the unintended consequences of their decisions.

The memory of the fallen, both friend and foe, haunted them. The faces of the innocent caught in the tangled web, the anguish of the manipulated and the despair of the willingly complicit– all these images haunted their sleep, their nightmares populated by the moral grey areas they had navigated with such ruthless efficiency.

Their love, once a refuge, became a battlefield. They argued, their exhaustion fuelling their frustrations. Warrick, grappling with the burden of guilt, questioned his behaviour and ignorance and pondered on the time wasted and the guilt of having his wife face the majority without him. He was tormented by images of innocent casualties, which might have been saved had he acted sooner and by questions that had no simple answers.

Still carrying the scars of her ordeal, Eleanor tried to maintain her resolve, reminding him of the greater good they had achieved. But even her unwavering faith was strained by the weight of their shared burden. The victory had come at a terrible price, and the moral cost was a burden they carried between them, silently, as their love faltered under the weight of unspoken doubts and immeasurable loss.

The world had been saved, but the battle within their own hearts and minds raged on, a silent war fought in the shadows of their victory, leaving them to wrestle with the unsettling truth that heroism and morality, in the face of overwhelming evil, might be more closely linked, irrevocably entangled. The reckoning was not only for the cabal but for themselves, a soul-searching journey that would continue long after the dust settled.

Consequences

The first sunrise after felt different. It wasn't just the absence of the oppressive grey haze that had clung to the country for so long, a haze born of manipulated despair. It was a lightness, a palpable shift in the air itself, a collective exhalation of breath held for too long. Yet, the lightness was fragile, like a newly hatched bird, vulnerable to the slightest gust of wind. The country, though freed from the immediate threat, was scarred.

Warrick stared out at the sky. Hazy blue replaced the greys of his memories. The grey of the endless rain, the grey of the perpetually overcast sky, the grey of the despair that had settled into the very marrow of his bones. Eleanor, beside him, her hand resting gently on his, mirrored his thoughtful gaze.
News reached them that their home had been destroyed in a fire, set by the cabal, of course, but it was staged as an electrical fire.

Eleanor stared out at the darkening sky, the familiar landscape now imbued with a layer of unsettling mystery.
 The "normalcy" the world presented was a thin veneer, a carefully crafted illusion masking the insidious reality of what they had faced.

One night, after a particularly tense argument, Eleanor found herself alone, staring out at the moonlit landscape. A new flashback hit her: a woman dressed in ancient robes, staring into the distance. The image was accompanied by a sense of urgency, of impending doom. The woman in the vision was holding a small, intricately carved wooden box. The symbol carved into the box felt familiar, strikingly similar to a symbol she'd seen in some of the leaked documents. The symbol represented a hidden energy source, one the cabal was desperately seeking. The vision vanished as quickly as it appeared, leaving Eleanor with an unsettling premonition of a looming threat.

The next morning, she approached Warrick with a new plan. She had spent the night meticulously piecing together the fragmented information, creating a timeline of the cabal's activities, from their earliest known experiments to their current operations. She had identified a pattern, a recurring motif suggesting the cabal's obsessive pursuit of a specific energy source. The wooden box in her vision, she believed, held the key. She needed to find it.

The cracks began appearing in the façade of victory, beginning with a phone call. It was Inspector Davies, his voice strained, his usual jovial tone replaced by a grim urgency. "Mrs. Vance," he began, his words clipped, "we've had... several incidents. Suicides. Not... typical suicides. The same pattern, the same... emptiness in their eyes. Like the ones we saw before we found your... device."

The carefully constructed dam of her relief was in full crumble. The time-travel machines hadn't just altered the past; they had poisoned the present. The Synarchy's influence, even with their primary weapons actively sought by authorities and destroyed, lingered, malevolent, infecting minds and leaving behind a trail of devastation. The faces of those she'd seen, their vacant stares, haunted her. They weren't just victims of circumstance; they were casualties of a war fought on a scale she was still trying to comprehend.

The next few days were a blur of police interviews, hushed conversations with government officials, and a growing sense of helplessness. The official line was vague, bordering on obfuscation – accidental overdoses, tragic accidents, unexplained psychological episodes.

Her husband, Warrick, was beside her, supportive, but the experience had shaken him to his core, the reality of their near-death experience settling upon him like a shroud. He tried to shield her from the growing wave of despair, but Eleanor couldn't escape it. Every news report, every hushed conversation, every anxious glance served as a grim reminder of the insidious legacy they'd inherited.

The investigation brought the authorities into contact with a network of whistleblowers, individuals who had previously brushed against the edges of the Synarchy's influence. A disgruntled tech expert revealed fragments of the Synarchy's technology – a complex system of algorithms designed to target specific individuals, subtly manipulating their thoughts and emotions, driving them to despair.

The Synarchy hadn't just used technology but harnessed ancient energies, weaving them into a tapestry of psychological manipulation and temporal distortion. Their goal wasn't merely to control individuals but to rewrite history to shape the future according to their twisted vision.

And even with the time machine being destroyed, the echoes of their actions resonated through their reality.

Eleanor found herself embroiled in a silent war, a battle fought not with weapons but with facts, with truth, with the sheer force of her will. She learned to navigate the shadowy world of government secrecy, the labyrinthine corridors of power, and the insidious manipulations of those who sought to bury the truth. She used her wit, her resilience, and her unwavering determination to unearth the truth and to ensure that the Synarchy's crimes didn't go unpunished. Her investigation, however, led to unexpected consequences, exposing corruption at the highest levels of government. The revelation that some government officials were complicit, even active participants in the Synarchy's schemes, was devastating for the public.

The public, still unaware of the full extent of the Synarchy's activities, remained vulnerable. Eleanor knew they couldn't simply stop at destroying the time machine. They had to expose the truth, even if it meant putting themselves in danger. The fight was far from over; it was just shifting into a new, more treacherous phase.

The weight of responsibility pressed down on her, the burden of countless lives hanging in the balance. She faced the prospect of a long, arduous battle, a fight against an enemy that could manipulate reality itself. Yet, within her, a quiet strength burned, fuelled by her love for her family, her loyalty to her friends, and an unwavering resolve to bring the Synarchy to justice.

One evening, while sifting through documents - Eleanor stumbled upon a series of coded messages. She recognised the style a variation of a cypher used by cryptographers during the Second World War. She contacted Wilson and Dr. Albright to take a look. Days and nights blurred into a concentrated effort to decipher the code.

The decoded messages revealed a chilling plan: the Synarchy intended to create a network of smaller, more mobile time-distortion devices. These would be far more discreet, easier to hide, and capable of subtly manipulating events over a wider area, influencing elections, markets, and even individual lives on a grand scale. The destruction of a couple of main machines had been a setback, but it was far from a defeat for The Synarchy. They were adapting, preparing for a new wave of influence.

Eleanor knew then they needed to act quickly. The fight wasn't just about exposing the Synarchy's crimes. It was about preventing their future plans. This realisation, however, came with a bitter taste. She understood now that this was not a simple crime that could be solved with a single arrest or the destruction of a single machine. The Synarchy, with its multiple heads, able to regenerate itself through an intricate network of influence, money, and power and never accountable.

They had won a battle, but the war wasn't over. She picked up the phone, the silver detonator-cigarette lighter cold in her hand, the chilling implications of the decoded messages swirling in her mind. The familiar comfort of their safehouse now felt like the eye of a storm, the calm before another, more dangerous, confrontation.

Unexpected

The phone rang, jarring Eleanor from the unsettling quiet. It was DCI Davies, his voice tight with a mixture of exhaustion and grim determination.

"It's… it's another incident," he said, his voice tight with apprehension. "In Geneva….it's… different. More focused, more targeted. And the victims…they're exhibiting…enhanced abilities. Strange reflexes, heightened senses…"

Warrick felt a cold dread creep into his heart. Enhanced abilities?

The targets seemed to be chosen randomly, scattered across the region - a scientist, a journalist, a housewife. Each displayed extraordinary new abilities. Some possessed superhuman strength; others demonstrated precognitive abilities. The common link was unclear, but the fear was palpable.

"We need everyone, and I mean everyone, to keep this under wraps for now, but we need your help."

"We've just uncovered they've got plans to build smaller time machines. We were going to send you the info to take it forward. Perhaps we can exchange." Eleanor realised she was entering the next phase.

"We're looking into that too. Send us what you have. It will no doubt be useful," he replied.

"There's also the matter of the Time Portals," she added. "You have the map of each location in the documents we handed you. They'll be using those to disappear. One is on my family's land, and you have my full permission to destroy it."

"Already have a team on those. I'll get the details from you as to the location on your land and thank you for your honesty. You could have used it for any number of purposes, but you chose to tell us. You are certainly different."

The investigation led them down a rabbit hole of international organisations, hidden laboratories, and shadowy figures operating in the darkest corners of the internet. They discovered that the Synarchy's technology, far from being destroyed, had been scattered, fragmented, and adopted by other groups. These groups were less focused on mass control and more interested in creating super-soldiers, manipulating individuals for their own ends.

The team were back at the Safehouse together for the next crisis.

The new technology, it was believed, wasn't based on time travel but on a different form of manipulation - something advanced, equally dangerous. It involved directly altering the human genome, unlocking latent potential in ways that were both disturbing and deeply horrific.

The officer, whose voice was tight with fear even through the encrypted channel, whispered about rumours of a new substance, codenamed "Project Stealth," a genetically engineered organism capable of rewriting human DNA, granting extraordinary abilities while simultaneously rendering the host susceptible to the whims of the creators. It was, he said, the next stage of evolution - an evolution controlled by those who sought to dominate.

Ralph began, "So their next step in our apparent evolution they've decided upon is none other than gene editing. I mean, if those in power can actually manipulate DNA, we're talking about a whole new level of oppression. If they twist our biology to serve their ends, we will end up with clones loyal to their cause. That would be abhorrent."

Ivor gestured animatedly as he wrapped his mind around the notion. "Imagine a machine built specifically to design humans according to a formula. That's one serious error in programming away from societal disaster! I mean, what if they end up with a 'perfect' human model who's completely incapable of independent thought?"

"Possibly their aim? There'd be no one to question anything ever again." Warrick said.

"Indeed. Genetic engineering for oppression isn't progress; it's a regression to tyrannical coercion." Agnes added.

"Ah, but what's a good dystopian plot without a band of rebels ready to upend the system? We can't just sit with our coffee cups and let them build a Brave New World, can we?" Barnaby interjected.

Eleanor nodded, "Now let's figure out how to stop them before they figure out how to stop us," a glint in her eyes.

It was a horrifying thought. The idea of creating superhumans who were mere puppets - no freedom, no will of their own - was a twisted perversion of humanity. And they couldn't let it succeed.

Warrick and Eleanor found themselves caught in a desperate race against time, trying to unravel the mystery behind Project

Stealth before it could spread further. They faced not only the challenge of identifying those responsible but also the daunting task of understanding how this new technology worked.

The information they uncovered was fragmented, hinting at a vast, complex network that stretched across continents. They learned of covert meetings in secluded mountain retreats, encrypted communications intercepted by shadowy intelligence agencies, and clandestine experiments carried out in hidden laboratories. The trail was a blind trail of red herrings, deliberate misinformation, and cryptic clues.

"We don't have the expertise in my unit, nor, if I'm honest, do I trust all of my colleagues. The corruption runs deep, and this is highly sensitive, as you know. Will you help?"

"We need to find out more about the DNA manipulation process they're using," Agnes said quietly, her voice firm despite her years. "From what we've learned over the years, they won't be giving them strength or intelligence without something sinister. They're aiming for something more."

As they learned more about the DNA manipulated humans, it became clear what their intentions were.

Their investigation led them to a remote property on a different continent, a place shrouded in myth and legend. Rumours spoke of a hidden research facility, a place where Project Stealth was being refined and weaponised.

DCI Davies organised the funds; they'd enter as tourists, an almost crime under international laws, but they had no choice. They needed to go over the heads of all due to the corruption and international implications.

Their investigation brought them face-to-face with the terrifying reality of the consequences of genetic manipulation and the human cost of unchecked ambition.

"These enhanced humans will be programmed - like living machines, obedient and incapable of rebellion," Eleanor said.

The creation of monstrous beings, humans twisted and warped by the organisms, their bodies and minds subject to the will of their creators.

Another mastermind – a ruthless scientist driven by a twisted vision of the future. He had envisioned a world ruled by genetically superior beings, a world free from weakness and imperfection. He had seen himself as a god, a creator of a new human race.

The cabal was vast and secretive, operating under layers of protection and deception.

Trevor and Ivor, both tech geniuses before and having developed some additional proficiency in all matters to do with tech, were the first to discover the vulnerability. Through careful tracing of digital breadcrumbs, they had found the entry point they could exploit: the facility's central command system had been designed for ease of access for certain high-ranking officials. It had a backdoor.

"We'll need to slip in undetected," Trevor murmured as he stared at the screen. "Once we're inside the system, we'll initiate a lockdown. We can override their security remotely. But we need to move fast."

DCI Davies, their new ally, raised an eyebrow. "How are we getting in without triggering alarms? They'll have a dozen countermeasures running the second we step foot in that facility."

Eleanor smiled. "We'll slip through their cracks," she said, her voice low and assured. "We won't be detected because they won't know we're coming."

We need to create a distraction. We'll create another crisis, something that demands their immediate response."

And so, their plan took shape.

For the next few hours, the team worked like clockwork. Trevor and Ivor set up false signals to simulate a massive cyberattack coming from an external threat. Ralph planted dead drops in key locations, triggering encrypted messages that implied an imminent breach in the facility's nuclear stockpile - a simulation so convincing that it would force their handlers to redirect their attention elsewhere.

Wilson, Agnes, Barnaby and Dr Albright crafted a story using their extensive knowledge of the cabal's history - a deep, historical narrative of rebellion and uprising. Using ancient symbols and cryptic messages, they linked them to a myth of an ancient revolution against the elite that mirrored the current moment, something the cabal could not ignore.

By the time they were ready to execute, Eleanor felt a calm settling over her.

Each of them stepped into their roles with practised ease. As the hours stretched into the evening, their carefully constructed illusion began to take form.

The abandoned military compound was far from any city centre, nestled deep within a forest. From the outside, it looked like any other forgotten installation – rusting fences, overgrown pathways, and the remnants of a past era. But beneath the surface, a carefully hidden technological empire thrived.

They entered through a series of tunnels, using the cabal's own outdated access points against them. The tunnel smelled of damp concrete and vegetation. They moved quickly, with Ivor leading the way, a quiet but steady force.

Trevor spoke softly into his earpiece. "I'm almost there. Once I trigger the cyberattack, the facility will go into lockdown. It's not a complete lockdown – simply enough to divert their attention."

Eleanor, a few steps behind, smiled slightly. "Perfect. It's a game of misdirection. The real trick will be getting inside the lab unnoticed."

The facility's security systems were sophisticated, but they weren't unbreachable.

As Trevor's signal triggered the first layer of deception, the sound of alarms in the distance confirmed their success. The cabal's attention shifted away from the perimeter, concentrating instead on the simulated threat of an external cyber attack.

The room was a flurry of activity on their screens as staff scrambled to verify the information, their focus now entirely on the new crisis.

The team moved through the halls undetected, slipping past guards too preoccupied with their screens to notice. They reached the central laboratory - sealed off with high-tech locks and surveillance – and with the chaos outside, the system was distracted and failed to register their presence.

Ivor was a step behind them, his fingers working furiously on his device. The final override was in place.

"It's done," he said as the lab's entry doors slid open silently.

Inside, the lab was sterile and cold, rows of dormant bio-tanks filled with the floating, mutated humans - the experiments that were meant to reshape humanity into something controllable. The organisms that would have rewritten the human genome, stripping people of free will and turning them into mindless, powerful drones, lay in a series of files on the computer terminal.

But the team wasn't here only to destroy. They were here to stop the process of any further production.

Ivor moved first, decrypting the data files with practised ease. Trevor began to plant false readings in the system's logs, ensuring that when the cabal's operatives reviewed their internal systems later, they would find nothing but corruption. Their plans would be sabotaged, but they wouldn't know how. No one would be able to trace back the origin of the breach.

"Can you stop the organisms's propagation?"

"Whatever it is," she said, her voice low, "it doesn't just alter DNA. It's a form of mind control. Once the organism enters into someone's bloodstream, they're no longer in control of their own body. The cabal takes over."

Elena, who had been scanning the room, spoke up. "We need to destroy it. All of it."

Trevor nodded. "I've reprogrammed their systems. The organisms will be as effective as splodge. Even if the organisms are in someone's bloodstream now, without the programming, they're useless."

"Now, let's destroy this lab and all its contents. All the organisms must be destroyed."

"I think I have just the thing for that." Trevor smiled.

The team ran out and stopped to watch as the lab went bang in a flash of light. The occupants ran around screaming, and all were escaping the soon-to-be collapsed underground building. Eleanor smiled, staying true to their values. The only damage they caused was to the cabal's plans and infrastructure.

The cabal was now blind. Their plans for a new human race, built on control and domination, had been undone. The organisms would never leave this facility, and the world would never know it had even existed. The arrests and prison sentences would follow with the sound of sirens they heard in the distance, courtesy of DCI Davies.

It was the beginning of something great - something the cabal could never have anticipated. They were no longer the hunters. They were no longer the ones shaping the future.

As they disappeared into the shadows, more of the cabal's empire, built on manipulation and fear, crumbled without a single shot being fired.

Davies and his team, meanwhile, were raiding properties. He said during the raid on a few of The Synarchy's properties - filled more with dusty occult paraphernalia than gleaming tech - they'd discovered a hidden compartment in one. Inside, nestled amongst ancient scrolls and cryptic diagrams, was a small, intricately carved wooden whistle. It was unlike anything Davies had ever seen. Initial analysis suggested it was far older than it appeared, possibly dating back centuries. More importantly, it was emitting a faint, almost imperceptible signal. "The signal," Davies continued, his voice low, "is unique. We've traced it to a series of underground tunnels, a network running beneath properties scattered through the countryside."

The underground tunnels proved to be a network stretching far beyond what anyone had initially suspected. The Synarchy had clearly been operating in the shadows for a considerable amount of time, meticulously building their network of deceit and manipulation. The tunnels were damp, claustrophobic, and filled with the eerie silence of forgotten places. The air felt heavy with the musty smell of earth.

Davies's team carefully navigated the tunnels. The deeper they went, the more unsettling the discoveries became. They found abandoned laboratories filled with half-finished experiments, unsettling devices humming with low, menacing energy. There were scattered notebooks filled with cryptic equations and disturbing sketches depicting distorted human figures. The whole atmosphere was chilling, hinting at the grotesque experiments that had been conducted within those subterranean chambers.

Finally, they reached the heart of the operation: a cavernous chamber that housed the main component of the time-travel machine, now significantly damaged but still pulsing with residual energy. Surrounding it were several deactivated control consoles and a vast array of strange, alien-looking technology.

The destruction of the main component of the time-travel machine was swift and decisive. With the main control unit disabled, the residual energy dissipated, leaving behind only a lingering hum and the chilling memory of what could have been.

But the aftermath was far from simple. The tunnels needed to be secured, the technology analysed, and the surviving members of The Synarchy apprehended. The investigation was far from over, but a crucial battle had been won.

A Happy Ending

"So," Davies began, his voice gravelly, "we've got a few of them, as far as we know for now. The leadership we're aware of is in custody, apart from Dr Evelyn Reed – the search is leading to dead ends. The technology… well, let's just say it's been thoroughly decommissioned. But there are still loose ends.."
Eleanor nodded, a familiar knot tightening in her stomach. The initial relief of victory was already fading, replaced by the unsettling feeling that something – or rather, someone - was still missing. The pieces of the puzzle, meticulously gathered, still didn't quite fit together. There were too many unanswered questions, too many lingering shadows.

"There's one thing," Davies continued, leaning forward, his gaze intense. "A name that keeps cropping up in the interrogation transcripts. A name that wasn't on any of our lists. A name that throws the whole thing into a new light."

He paused, letting the suspense hang heavy in the air. Eleanor waited, her heart drumming against her ribs. The quiet tension in the room was palpable, thick enough to cut with a knife. Winston, sensing the shift in mood, lifted his head, his ears pricked, and his eyes clouded with an unusual intensity.

"The name," Davies finally revealed, his voice low, "is Marcus Blackwood."
The name struck Eleanor like a physical blow. Blackwood. The Manor was Blackwood Manor. Unrelated?
"Who is he?" Eleanor asked, her voice barely a whisper.

Davies shook his head. "That's the mystery. He wasn't connected to the Synarchy directly, at least not officially. But his influence is all over their operations. Financial records, coded messages, even some of the technology – it all seems to lead back to him."

Days turned into nights, and the investigation continued.

Eleanor, driven by a persistent sense of unease, delved deeper into the enigmatic figure of Marcus Blackwood. She scoured historical records, interviewed old associates, and followed every lead, no matter how tenuous. Each piece of information she uncovered was more baffling than the last. Blackwood seemed to be a phantom, a ghost flitting through the edges of history, leaving only a trail of cryptic clues and unanswered questions.

Then, in a dusty archive hidden away in the local library, Eleanor stumbled upon a forgotten manuscript. It was a diary, penned in elegant handwriting, detailing the life and work of a reclusive scholar – a certain Marcus Blackwood. The entries, filled with complex equations, philosophical musings, and strange pronouncements, were cryptic and often incomprehensible. But one entry, tucked away amidst a discussion of temporal mechanics and quantum entanglement, sent a chill down Eleanor's spine. Marcus, of course, was the man she'd encountered whilst waiting for Esther in the cafe. The man who'd said he'd find her again.

It described a "counter-mechanism," a fail-safe designed to neutralise the Synarchy's time-travel device in case of catastrophic failure. Blackwood, it appeared, hadn't just been aware of the Synarchy's activities; he had been secretly working to counteract them, creating a hidden fail-safe designed to prevent the very disaster Eleanor had witnessed. The mechanism wasn't connected to the machine itself; it operated on a completely separate plane, utilising a principle Blackwood described as "entropic resonance."

Then came the revelation of unexpected heroism. The quiet, unassuming scholar had spent years discreetly working in the shadows, preparing for a contingency that most people wouldn't even consider.

The realisation struck Eleanor with the force of a physical impact. Marcus

Blackwood wasn't a villain; he was a silent guardian, a solitary knight battling the same foe. The Synarchy's defeat, it turned out, hadn't been solely due to their capture; Blackwood's counter-mechanism had been subtly neutralising the effects of the time-travel machine, preventing further catastrophic consequences. Their actions had hastened their capture, but Blackwood's quiet dedication had ensured the ultimate time machine's ultimate undoing and mitigated its devastating impact.

Eleanor felt a profound sense of admiration and gratitude for this unsung hero. She also felt a deep sense of responsibility.

Blackwood's sacrifice, his quiet dedication to saving the world from a threat he could not have imagined reaching its full potential, deserved recognition.

The manuscript also revealed another crucial piece of information - a hidden location in the countryside, where Blackwood had stored vital components for his counter-mechanism, ensuring its ongoing stability and efficiency.

Armed with this knowledge, Eleanor and Davies set out to secure this location, ensuring that Blackwood's legacy would live on, protecting the world from any future threats.

The resolution, however, wasn't simply about apprehending criminals and securing technology. It was about understanding the subtle interplay of human actions, the unexpected alliances that emerge in times of crisis, and the enduring power of quiet, unsung heroes. It was about recognising that even in the darkest times, hope can emerge from the most unexpected places, often from those operating silently in the background, quietly shaping the course of events.

The town, once steeped in the shadows of The Synarchy, began taking steps necessary for healing. The public, initially shaken and traumatised, slowly started to rebuild their lives. The eerie silence that had settled over the community was replaced by the gentle hum of daily life.

The images of panicked officials, their faces etched with a mixture of shock and shame, were plastered across social media outlets. The memes were savage, witty, and utterly cathartic, reflecting the public sense of dark relief.
But the liberation wasn't without its cost. The aftermath was chaotic, emotionally charged, and complex. The world had to grapple with the full extent of the manipulation. Lives had been destroyed, families shattered, and trust broken. The economic repercussions were devastating, and the psychological fallout was still unfolding.

The withdrawal from the cabal's mind control manifested in various ways - some experienced intense headaches, others suffered from debilitating nightmares, and others felt a profound sense of disorientation and confusion as their minds struggled to adjust to the absence of external control.

Hospitals were overwhelmed, which led neighbours to help neighbours, communities rallied, and strangers offered support. The shared trauma, though horrific, forged an unexpected bond of resilience. The world was reeling, but there were signs of positivity.

The initial wave of liberation was chaotic. People stumbled, not literally, but mentally. Years of subtle manipulation had warped their perceptions, their desires, and their very sense of self. Their disruption to the cabal's nefarious plans hadn't magically erased the years of insidious programming and torment. It was like waking from a long, strange dream, the lingering effects blurring the line between reality and the carefully constructed illusion the cabal had spun.

One moment, a man might be consumed by a desperate urge to buy a new car he couldn't afford. The next, he'd be staring blankly at the advertisement, the desire inexplicably gone, replaced by a gnawing sense of unease, questioning his own motivations. A woman, previously driven to near-suicidal despair by the amplified negativity of the dark energies, found herself overwhelmed by a sudden, almost painful sense of freedom, paralysed by the sheer weight of choices she hadn't been allowed to make for years.

Another positive change emerged in the shift in the collective consciousness, a subtle yet palpable shift towards a deeper appreciation of human connection, of the importance of love and compassion towards each other and all life on the planet. In its perverse way, the Conspiracy had served as a catalyst, forging a stronger sense of community and a collective commitment to safeguarding the well-being of all. A collective mindset of a new awareness of personal responsibility for the

welfare of all. It reinforced the understanding that individual actions have far-reaching consequences and that collective action is essential
to combating the insidious forces of oppression and tyranny.

For many, however, the world still felt strangely alien, a place they no longer fully recognised.
Eleanor watched the parallels unfolding, acutely aware of their complex reality. It wasn't a simple physical detox; it was a journey to rehabilitation and the psychological and emotional rewiring of millions. The cabal's control hadn't been just technological; it had been a systematic dismantling of individual agency, a meticulously executed erosion of free will.

Restoring that was proving more difficult than anyone had anticipated.
Warrick was immersed in the logistical challenges. Food supplies, disrupted by the conspiracy's deliberate sabotage, needed replenishing. Infrastructure, weakened by years of neglect (a deliberate tactic by the cabal to keep society vulnerable), had to be repaired. It was a Herculean task, and yet, there was a sense of purpose that permeated the air, a palpable energy born of collective responsibility. It was a stark contrast to the apathy and despair that had defined the era. Despite his initial disbelief, Warrick found himself swept up in the tide of this renewed hope, working tirelessly alongside Eleanor and their unlikely band of heroes and Winston always by their side. Eleanor's inherited land and property, including their safe house, were donated to the rehabilitation project and turned into crop farms and proper education centres to provide stable jobs and support those who'd lost everything. The projects were run by the team who were closer than ever, creating,

designing and pushing for a peaceful society. They promoted media literacy and critical thinking, empowering individuals to resist manipulation and misinformation. They inspired others to become active participants in the fight against injustice. Their message was simple yet powerful: vigilance, scepticism, and unwavering belief in the power of truth were the ultimate weapons against those who sought to control and manipulate.

Eleanor witnessed a former stockbroker, once driven by ruthless ambition, now working at one of their farms, his eyes filled with a newfound empathy and a sense of genuine remorse for his past actions. A young woman, previously addicted to social media, a puppet dancing to the rhythm of algorithmic manipulation, now sat quietly in a library, immersed in a book, finding solace and meaning in the simple act of reading. These small victories were like tiny sparks, illuminating a quiet, personal redemption within her.
However, the road to recovery wasn't without its challenges.
There were those who found the return of true free will overwhelming and struggled to navigate a world without the cabal's reassuring (though manipulative) influence. Others, burdened by the memories of their actions while under the cabal's control, found themselves grappling with immense guilt and shame.
The world was recovering from the immense weight of its past, and the path forward was far from clear, but the commitment to building a fairer, more just society was undeniable.

Governments were forced to be transparent and accountable. But the shadows lingered. Not all members of the Synarchy were apprehended. Some slipped away, disappearing into the anonymity of the digital world, ready to plot their next scheme.

They were facing an enemy that was not just powerful but also timeless, an enemy that existed beyond the conventional understanding of evil. The fight, Eleanor knew, wasn't over. The restoration of free will was a victory, but it was only the first step in a longer, more complex battle for the future of humanity.

Eleanor had also found a deep appreciation for the quiet dedication of those who operate behind the scenes, shaping the world in ways we rarely recognise.
She was willing to heed her grandmother's wisdom to know God in this lifetime, and for that, she needed to first find and understand God.

"Do you think we'll ever truly be free?" Eleanor asked, her voice barely audible. The question hung in the air, heavy with unspoken fears and uncertainties. They'd faced the darkness and emerged, but the darkness still clung to the edges of their lives, casting long, menacing shadows.

Warrick took her hand, his touch a silent reassurance.

The final chapter was not an ending but a beginning. The fight against unseen threats continued, but Eleanor, armed with wisdom gained from her ordeal, felt better equipped to face the future.
She understood that true victory doesn't reside in the absence of darkness but in the unwavering light of hope and courage that shines even in the deepest shadows and within the indomitable human heart. The memory of Marcus Blackwood, the quiet scholar who had saved the world without ever seeking recognition, would forever serve as a reminder of this truth.

“I'm wondering how you are Eleanor, and how is your heart?”
Eleanor smiled. “Still hopeful.”
“Ahh, well, now that makes me hopeful too,” Penelope said.

She stopped typing there; her story, their story, would survive through the ages and serve as a warning. Perhaps she'd even read it in her next life - a smile formed on her lips at the thought.

Appendix

The story is fictional.

The appendix would have contained a selection of coded messages intercepted during the investigation, along with their deciphered translations. However, due to their sensitive nature, all were redacted and have since been removed to protect the sanity of anyone attempting to understand the Synarchy's bizarre communication style.